The Report of Mr. Charles Aalmers

and other stories

The Report of Mr. Charles Aalmers
and other stories

by Matthew Pungitore

2021

BOOKBABY
7905 N. CRESCENT BLVD. PENNSAUKEN, NJ 08110

The Report of Mr. Charles Aalmers and other stories
Written by Matthew Pungitore
Contact the author at: matthewpungitore_writer@outlook.com
Published by BookBaby

Cover art by SHAWN SLOWBURN

Book Design and Interior Book Design by BookBaby

Author Photo taken by Briana Pungitore

Printed in the United States of America
Published 2021
First Printing, 2021

(Print) ISBN 978-1-09834-708-6
(E-Book) ISBN 978-1-09834-709-3

BookBaby
7905 N. Crescent Blvd. Pennsauken, NJ
08110

With endless love, I dedicate this book to my nonno and nonna.

Contents

Acknowledgments

My sincere appreciation goes to Jesse Abraham Lucas, David Eyk, and Frank Ormond; while they did not help me write this book, their friendship gave me confidence, so I wanted to thank them for all those times when they offered me suggestions and when they helped me understand some literary practices. Jesse, David, and Frank bestowed unto me an air of camaraderie; thus, I hope to express my heartfelt thanks to them for being so cordial. To these three, I here leave this message: "Thank you for the friendly encouragement and conversation."

SHAWN SLOWBURN created the artwork for the cover of this book. It was a pleasure communicating and consulting with Shawn Slowburn, whose skills I highly recommend. From the great depths of my heart, I would like to thank SHAWN SLOWBURN for creating such a magnificent cover art for me. I look forward to the possibility of communicating and consulting with Shawn in the future.

Deep respect must be given to BookBaby Publishing and the entire BookBaby team. They have always been incredibly helpful and kind. What BookBaby does for writers like me is undoubtedly important.

For a lifetime of kindness and benevolence, I would like to say genuine thanks to my amazing grandmother Maria Mazza Marcella. To my kindhearted grandfather Mario Pasquale Marcella, I pray we both enjoy many joyful tomorrows with each other; he has always been so strong, comic, and hard-working. They both will always have a loving place in my heart and mind.

Family will always be a large part of my life. My parents have always been by my side, and they have continually done more than their best for our family. My sister is a star of brightness and cheer that has kept me surviving onward. For my beloved father—Giovanni Pungitore—I offer warm thanks and fond reverence; his generous and fervent spirit has emboldened me through difficult times. For my witty sister—Briana Giovanna Maria Pungitore—mortal words could never express the unfathomable love I have for her. For my ingenious mother—Juliana Marcella Pungitore—my love and adoration for her is unending, and I will cherish her beyond the limits of time.

The Preface

This book, this anthology, started as a collection of all the short stories and things that I had written over the course of a year or more but failed to get published anywhere. I had sent them off for submission to magazines and other such presses or people looking for stories, but no one wanted to take them. Thus, this collection began as just a bundle of all my stories that were unwanted and rejected. Aye, the sad and honest cold truth of it all; yet, misery doth have habit allowing something beautiful and hopeful to grow in the spirit of those strong enough or wise enough or lucky enough to understand, to want it. I adored every single story I had written; I saw their value, saw how they could help enhance my favorite horror genres: stories of the Gothic, the weird, and the fantasy. I had been telling people to write what they love, and I loved these stories, so I should want to share these pieces of myself. Each of them clawed at my soul and dared be unleashed as I read them! I had to read aloud at times! I didn't want to abandon them, nor erase. I pushed them into this book and left them as they were, more or less, small adjustments were made, getting rid of or changing the absolutely unnecessary bits. Very slight changes were made to the stories to make them flow better or look better with this anthology. Then, I wrote new stories, ones I knew would complement the other stories. And I wrote more, always with the idea to keep every story unique and detached. After this, I created newer tales and newer stories; next, I added them into this book. After, I realized that this book was now a collection of old and new stories, old and new parts out from my imagination.

Readers should look at each of these stories as a separate narrative unconnected to any of the other stories in this collection; however, I wrote them in a way so that readers can also be able to see where the stories might blur into one another, see the places in the stories where the universes within them might overlap and mingle. One could say that each story does share a doorway to another story of this anthology, that those stories sometimes intersect or interweave with one another. Nevertheless, each story can be seen to have nothing to do with any of the other stories appearing here in this compilation. One would be correct in saying that each story in this book is standalone. But, I would also have readers remember to think of it like the stories are in parallel universes circling around, and at times even into, one another. This is something each reader will have to decide for themselves as individuals and as explorers. Books and stories like these are connections and communications creating webs linking readers, authors, minds, and dreams.

Why Horror, the weird, and the dark? Why concern with these? They are all facets, elements I find fitting and sympathetic to my ways of being and conveyance; the literature of horror and the macabre and the Gothic is fun, for me at least. Horror, and the act of reading such works, brings time for reverence, for solemnity, for gravity; it brings a refreshing isolation, or a type of cathartic abasement, that revives and is individualistic while also creating empathy or sympathy or kinship for the sufferings and evils and mysteries of ourselves and others and what we think is reality. Horror and works of the uncanny open a pathway to the sublime, to find awe and respect for life, for living, for the dead, for the unknown—it is powerful and almost unexplainable. It is weird—and even I don't dare say I can fully understand, but that is why it is important to keep telling and creating these kinds of stories.

It has been my objective to evolve the lightning of all that is Gothic, the weird, and the fantasy with a pulp-like mindset and pulp-like air—pulp-style to add that attitude of fun and thrill only it knows best—and mutate all these genres together with pieces of myself and my imagination, to create worlds of words and dreams and narratives that can be experienced and read by others who, like me, share a love and affinity for the macabre, the gruesome, and the weird. Each of these genres, to me, is like its own language of emotions and memories. Fiction, even genre itself, must change to become stronger for future writers, and I want to help it grow, because I feel kinship to it. I want this new form to reflect a new age of sublime and romance, one that I hope I can create so it suits my tastes and moods and wishes. I want to be one of those who updates these genres—the Gothic and the weird and the dark—into those which better help the expression and furthering of my ideas and my creative spirit.

As a writer, I almost feel like it is my quest to make a new sublanguage, a dialect, or a sub-vernacular; to think of new ways to use English grammar and American English grammar, and to form new thought-patterns, to make that which could bring all upon new vistas of intensity and passion. I have wanted to see and to create a transformed wordsmithery, a finer literature, and more fun fictional works, ones that may be lifted to new sublimes, erupting new and better ways to think and feel about how to tell stories, about how to think and feel about art and literature and beauty. Especially with this book, I have tried to write in a way that my readers may understand best, but I had wished to use old writing styles and to mix it with a development of new or unique styles of using many different types of words, English grammar, my own kind of blend of different languages, and different types of syntax, all while bringing these techniques back to traditional and antiquated modes. Some of the stories in this collection show this attitude or characteristic more than others, some might not show it at all, but it was certainly something I was thinking about more and more after I wrote each story one after the other after the other.

When existing words were found wanting, when common or popular words of English were deficient, I desired new English words to help propel the expression of my evolving imagination. Thus, I have within these stories made an attempt to create and stitch together new English words and things, which, as far as I know, as far as I am currently aware, are new words created from my imagination, words I created with inspiration and influence from words belonging to Old English, Middle English, British English, American English, Irish, Italian, and from many more languages. Of course, there is no way for me to know if the English words I created are the same or very similar to words from non-English languages or some different language system I'm not familiar with. To the best of my abilities, I have tried to make sure my words are unique, interesting, and original. Here are some of my creations: "famigliarch," "neromealltach," "metafeoil," "wynnsyth," "wynsithen," "aljiswyghte," "eilewiht," "sembosemmcyn," "elbosum," "hwondhyt," "mia-neachyt," "ealulych," and "wergianiht." How splendid it would be if one day in the future I could see these new words, my words, in an actual English-language dictionary. Could such a thing ever happen?

A writer can dream. Are books and stories not dreams?

Of course, I also had a lot of fun creating unique and bizarre new names for my own monsters, otherworldly entities, and such too.

When it comes to making new English-language words or trying to establish a unique way of story-expression, I have tried to consider interesting syntax-quirks of many different languages and mix them with hues of my favorite languages. It has been like trying to create something new while also trying to resurrect something old. And yet, concerning all this, always I feel as though I fall. Perhaps I have failed. I could use only what I could and what I knew or understood. I am no master of language or words; I have not actually made a whole new system of language, but I will never stop trying to elevate the English language, to elevate the way English, these words, can be used to tell better stories and express ourselves richen. Again—not all of my stories in this collection were written so byzantine or so florid, and some I wrote simply or conventionally; that might just be something for readers to decide for themselves individually. There is certainly some experimentation happening in this anthology; that's for sure. I just hope it can satisfy.

Clarity, skepticism, and realism are absolutely important tones within this book, but they are not everything. Mote it be a thunder-charged tempest, my work, which doth clash bizarre, esoteric, eldritch, ecclesiastical, occult, mysticism, and grotesque elements. My work, may it bestow every fright and thrill for which any couldst ever perchance beseech. Henceforth, may it be pathway suffice to sensations sublime and weird uncanny!

The best for ye, dear readers, mine ardent wish be. My hope is ye enjoy thyselves my anthology.

Godspeed,

Matthew Pungitore
Hingham, MA
Saturday, October 31, 2020

(10/31/2020)

The Report of Mr. Charles Aalmers
and other stories

The Report of Mr. Charles Aalmers

A Note on the Text

"Never go in a cemetery at night," was the overall warning I received from the old Gothamite housewives and hoary groundskeepers I met while rambling all around and through New York City, strolling up and down the Hudson River, and visiting many of the villages and cities within reach. I'd met one or two New Yorkers and some sightseers who told me rumors about the hellhounds and barghests that torment anyone caught in a graveyard after nightfall. One rumor caught my attention aflame—it was said that, every so often, someone would get chased out by the fiends haunting the graveyard of Dubhdris Abbey in Tarrytown. After the vandalism of the Claretta van der Veen tomb, some suspected not mortal villainy but something far older. Even the wizened monks of that abbey, who told me to ignore the rumors, could not hide their pale hints, and I heard one suggest they'd seen a daemonic canid upon the lych-gate.

At dusk, I snuck into the forbidden portion of the graveyard of Dubhdris Abbey and prowled its tombs and catacombs; as I did, I came through the underground murk of a Gothic crypt where I picked up a ghastly report, clearly one written by a mad man, but of historical import. I would've collected the other books beside it, but I fled when I saw the truth of this place and the rumors! Coming for me were teeth and long fleshy tendrils of a wolfish abomination! That many-legged nightmarish horror, a monster mostly inde-scribable, almost devoured me! Now I present what I brought back from the crypt beneath Dubhdris Abbey: the report of Mr. Charles Aalmers.

With deepest regards,

Edgar DeWitt

The Report of Mr. Charles Aalmers

I

Mr. Charles Aalmers—the name of thy much-obliged narrator for this gruesome yarn, and I am he, he who came up against true yet unjustifiable things, now writes of them here in the following report, a harrowing report of which I doubt many would believe in any regard.

Thus by this manuscript shall I bloody well recount of that precise series of experiences, sights, and imagining responsible for the crushing of my comfort and the ruin of my past preconceptions of reality, which demolished mine old faith to void-flung dust; any hope for mankind's existence abandoned.

O how I jostle with that bleak sentiment, which doth yell anathema to my entirety!

A foin at this tenebrosity! Prithee, return me to oblivious days not scourged nor flogged by interrupting reminders or memories morbific!

Whilst I now feign faith and conviction in an omnific Godhead and lawful rightness, which are myopic yet cheery folderols mankind ought never to abandon lest we of this earth truly desire a hastening to annihilation, I can never return to that Jovian empire of dignity; no rationality nor salvation exists outside the feeble barricades and faint simulations we tearfully fabricate. Humans were never meant to plumb reality without nepenthean delusion afore their minds.

After seeing now how futile all humanity's treasures be, how unavailing our grandiosity, how meager have been our empty minds and vacant vessels, only now do I cling tighter and cherish harder mortal works of splendor, passions, and morality, works given forms, which we mortals of upright society believe they ought to take or manifest: these distractions keep together sanity, that frail potation, before the doom of truth making itself a nemesis against our wish for grace and ideals. Death is the forgetting overseer, the absentminded eternity of our existence. Overshadowed am I by a grim weird. An omen cosmic. Exemplary verity, shifty and bilking, takes intolerable property one must retch or else resign from humankind; for the sole certitude of a human is that oppressing vertigo signaling our futility, a reminder that all humanity can achieve or conceive is half-truth doddering on indifferent nihility. An uncanny ancient doth jeopardize and sway all reality and human life from behind and beneath the veneer of the day-to-day, expected routines of our flimsy mortal lifestyles. That old horror doth not hide, it simply cannot be perceived by any save the mad or depraved, and its subtle workings are only scarcely deciphered when any act to defy it is already useless.

It has been months since I lit black candles as dirges knelled, and the dead march let fly shadows bereaving. I oft have visited her tomb, she whom I had once loved sincerely from the first day we had met! O how miserably I mourn for her! Bound shall I always be in hating chain and miserable love to her: Claretta van der Veen!

To explain myself full, I must impart this story of our friendship and of her death.

II

Yea, and now this: on how the moral, psychological, and mortal hazard began to intrude upon my life. 'Twas when I had begun travailing between several agencies and guilds as an antiquarian, medievalist, and folklorist. At a fit age of forty, and working out of a stately office in Tarrytown of New York, valued was I for my contacts, expertise, and informants concerning matters of antiquity, classical folkways, and European history: rewards and proud marks of my many years verily sacrificed in devotion to a part of history that must survive. Even then, as now, was I most preoccupied with preserving relics and remains once belonging to villeins, cottars, thanes, vassals, knights, and clerics of Scottish, French, English, and Italian peoples who had lived during the Middle Ages.

As Claretta and I had been working together for a few years, I had seen how she had been, in life, so warmhearted and reliable. She had used to read eld fables to me and had always been eager to invite me to join her on expeditions. In addition, she and I would sing together in private or while taking walks outdoor.

Aye, at times, Claretta could be oddly offish. There were instants I had been reminded of that aspect to her personality. She had used to say that she was not comfortable with intimacy, that she was not suited for amours or amorous relationships; so, I dreaded her spurn and did not want to flirt or reveal my unrequited love.

Alas! My true self had never found an opportunity to front her! I had never known a way to express my devotion for her! All hope of that happening dashed and burned the second she had told me she was to be betrothed to another, a wealthy man named Luciano, whom she had known since childhood.

I then began to suspect she had only been feigning unease at romantic intimacy all along as a way to keep me away. Claretta's company and demeanor were the red of my heart. Her gilt rays I still had want of for the sanguine garden of my hopes and dreaming. Bitter and regret spoiled her from my memories, yet more still, in contradiction, I relished her, for we had been on outstanding adventures together, ones of which I know did good for my character and mind.

Soon after, I had been hired to investigate a medieval crypt in France that had been opened up and destabilized by storm and earthquake. Several lists had been mailed to me with instructions on how I was to report on the presence, condition, and arrangement of the precious valuables and guests interred. My good friend and auxiliary historian Tewodros came to help, and Claretta joined us.

Many days and nights passed here in study and toil, and we slept little. One night, under that Gothic vault made we a most magnificent discovery, one which demanded hours of research and study: a hefty illuminated manuscript of the medieval manner and Gothicism. It had been bound and fixed with schorl-decorated plates of gold; opals were fixed around the corners of the front and back covers by silver mountings; pearled edging joined obsidian gemstones; and the front panel boasted an ivory bas-relief which portrayed undead, skull-grinning chevaliers under Gothic arches overseen by Christ in the clouds encircled by Scorpius and cherubim. Many of the leaves offered designs of Gothic cathedrals and crenelated castles furnished with crockets, flying buttresses, rose windows, gargoyles, quatrefoils, and tracery. There survived in the book an abundance of art of Gothic, Teutonic, Carolingian, and Ottonian cultures; there too were spots of Runic, Frankish, and other mysterious Germanic handwriting beside rubrics and illustrations denoting their respective heritages.

Most baffling of all were the volume's backmost sections containing subdivisions of mathematical equations; unexplainable chapters on ominous astrology; treatises on the auspicious or cataclysmic capabilities existing yet hidden in the appropriate or improper employment of geometry of the non-Euclidean and the maddening kinds; and sheets devoted to depictions of inexpressible incarnations and how to invoke their unknowable laws.

I must not forget to mention this book's equally atypical fables, legends, and chivalric romances written in an arcane, unknown, and vulgar version of medieval French; the handwriting evoked a sort of weird and spooking patois with characters and symbols of ill-bred harshness far too uncomfortable and unbearable to be uttered to exactitude by sophisticated human vocal cords.

Claretta found in it an Arthurian legend, and to us, we three athrill, posthaste read she aloud from that tome unimagined. The following is the tale, written in that cryptic dialect of Old French, that she read—

III

The romance started with the victorious wars and militaristic triumphs of a King Regulus and his horsemen gallant who defeated Saracens and barbarians from the east. He became a protective, caring master of his small kingdom. In respect and great attachment towards the beauty and splendor of his dominion was the king captivated. Honest and wholesome he believed his subjects to be. His territory—its earth, mountains, water, sky, wind, woodlands, and the fauna—the noble leader adored, aware his great kingdom was so made as reward for faith in the Demiurge and for friendship among himself and the tellurian numina of his region. To keep the lesser deities of his domain mild and tame had the Almighty commanded this good king.

A goddess, Princess Jorunn, ruled the night sky above the kingdom of King Regulus. For her would the king sing and compose rosy-tender poetry, wooing courtly, anything for the night-sky princess, whom the king loved with all his being. Princess Jorunn, nightly courted by King Regulus, approved of his gallantries and politeness.

Heaven saw Jorunn had birthed Regulus' son, Algautr, and warned of this to an envious queen of night. Blackest punishment demanded, out of green insecurity, the spiteful queen so very repellent. An old she-wolf heard the queen commanding her giant bats to capture Regulus, Jorunn, and Algautr. The wolf ran to Regulus with the news, but the cackling bats had already taken Jorunn. Afeard of the wroth night-queen's cunning, Regulus gave infant Algautr to the she-wolf to bring to heroic Arthur for protection. Regulus and his army battled the night-queen horror, but her silken webs of curses, girding the king and his men, condemned them to wretched forms of lycanthropy. Now as her night wolves, they did serve the jealous hag. The wolf-men destroyed their once-beautiful kingdom and slaughtered all within. Jorunn, chased by giant bats, was punished to spin around the ruins and commit it to a prison eternal-black.

Arthur met the she-wolf and protected Algautr. He and his knights attempted several attacks on the night-queen, but none could penetrate the darkness around the ruins, which the queen used to hide. Arthur decided he would raise Algautr to become a knight. Some years later, Arthur told the lad about his family and that it would be his destiny to bring justice to the land once ruled by his father, King Regulus.

As night passed, the jealous hag of night infiltrated the minds of Arthur, Algautr, and all who might stand to oppose her; and she used the dreams to make all forget her and Regulus' kingdom. This technique took many months, sapping her blood and much of her strength, which weakened the night queen, trapping her in sleep deep and terrible, but her curses and commands would continue to obscure her; soon, all would forget her and leave her in her misery undisturbed. One day, the curses would have to dwindle, and for that was Jorunn waiting.

More years flew, and many battles did Algautr share alongside Arthur. At eighteen years—with a puissance of archery, tilt, equitation, and swordsmanship, Algautr demonstrated on the battlefield a high caliber potency. Sought for was the partnership of this handsome man-at-arms, for rounds, vociferous dances, and carols, by dint of the covetous grasping of bonny dames and noblewomen innumerable who for him swooned unnoticed by their noble husbands.

Algautr fought beside Arthur and his chivalrous knights to stop the nefarious-bloody armies of Modred. Though his armies were defeated, Modred himself proved an adversary too powerful and brimmed of the utmost roguish-cunning. Black-clad Modred's heavy strikes would throw Algautr down each time their steel came to blows. At the end of their battles, Modred and Arthur backed away each time, with both sides facing heavy casualties.

Algautr survived, and he gained renown for facing Modred and helping Arthur. At a banquet, Algautr's eyes for a second met the look of Lady Maren as she passed, and he instantly fell in love. After that, he would not eat without tasting her affection, knowing she was not at his side. He feared terrible he should die of her absence. He would not see her again until the next spring, when at a festival they did share a gaze. His singing did nothing to impress Maren, and she refused to speak with him.

Modred sent a horde of brigands to capture Lady Maren and her sisters. Sir Algautr rode after them, found the thieves' lair, and single-handedly saved the three lovely sisters. For all this, Algautr had become their guardian and had won his knighthood. Lady Maren and her two sisters, all three coquettish beauties being eighteen and already married, would now flirt with him most out of all their devotees.

Secretly, as the world slept, Sir Algautr and Lady Maren would dally in hiding beside the ruins of an old, forgotten kingdom, which was now only ever a vague warning on the tongues of overly superstitious wives and their oft-sensitive children. It had always been a place obscured by black clouds and dark mist. All across this place were shadows so deep, rumors had whispered, that they were, in truth, fiend-loosened gateways to netherworlds that no mortal should explore, unheard of places guarded by hellhounds in sunlight-hunting shadows, which did eerily linger all through daytime.

Of these rumors, Sir Algautr was not afraid and believed in them not a tad. He had been meeting Lady Maren, she had been keeping these nocturnal appointments a secret from her husband, at the outskirts of this gossip-haunted site for many seasons, and nothing ill had ever taken spectral shape. Forsooth, something ill-strange about the night-air of this spot did bless Sir Algautr with a soothing melancholy, as if he was reuniting with someone dearest who can stay not long enough; such bracing emotions did burgeon the love he carried for Lady Maren.

She wanted never to shame in public or to leave her husband, but she had known no devotion from the spouse, and so she had long ago accepted to enter the fashionable yet controversial lifestyle of courtly love, a life she knew would mean her being divided in secrecy between two worlds, one of the mundane and one of noble passion.

Sir Algautr wanted more than kisses and favors for his gifts and poems to her. This made Maren feel more shame, for she did not want to be a heavy sinner, and she then fled from him for many months.

Algautr only won her back to him by singing to her at night from outside her window and by sending romantic letters under her door. The knight needed her beauty and validation to keep him in equilibrium with the world. His bravery and devotion was remarkable, and such love was admirable, for she knew how easy it would be for him to be caught romancing a married woman so brazenly, and she knew she could not live without his vigor.

One night, while the two were at the dark ruins and looking at the above stars, a giant bat swooped down and took Lady Maren deeper into the dark and misty wreckage. Sir Algautr chased but could not pass through a wide wall of gushing shadows behind which the blood-drainer had taken her. Nothing would do it damage, it so seemed to the brave knight; and so, he tried to climb it, but, each time he did, the wall stretched up to slap him with black gales which chomped his weapons and armor.

The dark wall yawned, revealing great whirlpools of blackness. Sir Algautr crossed himself. With every fiber of his faith and flesh, the knight trusted in the promise of redemption; bravery reminded Sir Algautr that nothing could block the way of one who follows the Trinity. Immediate after, forth those bowels Plutonian emerged beautiful hands of soft moonlight. Algautr held them, and they pulled him into the void.

As the hands moved up to his face, he remembered his mother Jorunn and could see her floating in light. Her son's bravery and hope had freed her at last. She offered him a sword made out of thick locks of her hair and of her teardrops. He gripped its hilt and saw it was made of obsidian-like ice and moon-dust held together with an unexplainable fortitude and ironlike component; the blade was a shaft of starlight-mottled dark energy with veins of hot steel. Only her son Algautr could ever wield this weapon, and now he had finally become worthy of joining its destiny.

Now he found himself on the other side of the shadow-wall, in a realm of corpse-encrusted fog. Sir Algautr used the brand to put down the swarms of giant bats and the legions of wolves pursuing his mother. With her help, he could fly to seize all his enemies. With his strikes came the silence of absolute purity and the supremacy of purging flood. That calamitous brand unleashed a Titan of vengeance, wreaking and annihilating the armies of the queen of night. His deluge washed away the corpse-blighted ruins and banished the otherworld-shadow wall.

Regulus attacked his son, and they fought on a large hill. Algautr stabbed Regulus' leg, and the wolf-curse was then removed off him. His wolf form became a black pelt with cobweb lining, and Regulus became a man again. Algautr was shocked to see this transformation. Jorunn would not let him kill his father, King Regulus. She told her son everything that had caused their separation and despair, about his father, and about the night-hag empress who had separated them.

Regulus gave the pelt to Algautr, knowing only his son, a demigod, could master its rage. Jorunn tended to Regulus' injury while their son searched for Lady Maren. Algautr found a cave from where he heard her screams. In this underworld, his sword provided light, and the pelt gave night-vision. In a cavern, he found the wicked and treasonous Modred consulting with a gigantic black widow, the queen of night. The massive spider, emitting a most sickening and smug purring, clutched Lady Maren. Modred, bargaining for Maren, revealed that he had murdered Maren's husband this night.

Algautr made dark his blade, and he moved with total silence, so they did not hear him or sense him there. However, as a chivalrous man, he revealed himself with a great booming shout, "Release Lady Maren!"

Instant was the cowardly spider vanished, as was Maren. Sir Algautr's blade, now radiant, terrified the old creature.

Modred laughed evil and drew his villainous sword. "I shan't be bested by an adulterous pretender, demigod abomination! My blade and I, we have tasted blood tonight and shall afresh upon the morrow after this punishment I plunge through the heart of failed Arthur, my dearest father, and his table of blackguards, coxcombs who elevate codes of Men before codes of God!"

"False knight and traitor, Modred," said Algautr. "Arthur and I have stopped thee and thine armies before. Arthur made for every man, every woman, and every child a rare future of hope! Selfish twit and knave thou art! Naught wilt thou accomplish for thy poor thievery!"

"A future of hope for every child? What of those babes he stole and butchered to be certain he could be rid of me? When he feared the prophecy which stated his unknown son would one day take his precious kingdom, he murdered everyone's sons, those he thought could have been me; remember, he did not know who his bastard was or what I looked like. Arthur lets his friends take his wife while he sleeps with other women. And thou speak to me of theft? We are monsters, thou and I. Let us have our fill of blood and death!"

Naught more was said between these two warriors who now leapt and darted about the cavern chamber. The walls and vault cracked from the terrifying clashing of their brands enraged, both combatants only becoming more powerful with the growing intensity of their fight. From their blades striking the floor, the world did thunder. Prolonged and bitter, each strike and lash producing rivers and fireballs, earth-shattering was the grievous combat, which unleashed the trapped beings of flame to erupt the mountains with volcanic devastation and opened the deep water below to gurgle up and deluge the land.

Mudslides and earthquake created enormous wide rifts which now divided Modred and Algautr. The demigod of night knew Lady Maren's safety was more important than this titanic conflict. The dark traitor knew that punishing Arthur's decadence was more important than risking his life here among the gods, and if he should die, he contemplated, he would rather it be after Arthur could see not the light of day as well. Looking into Algautr's far-away eyes, Modred thought about what the son of King Regulus had said about Arthur's kingdom of hope, but Arthur had spoiled that hope with allowing corruption, sin, and hypocrisy to take the reins of destiny. After all, Algautr had only reminded sad Modred of exactly why 'twas necessary to spill Arthur's blood and claim his life.

"There are too many things in this world which should have never been, which can never be explained," whispered star-doomed Modred, already riding off to front his father.

Algautr, seeing now the spider flee, ran after it into a near forest. He moved to high land where the flood reached not. Lady Maren was now dying from the queen's spider-bite. Algautr rived the beast, thus killing the queen of night who had cursed his parents long ago. Algautr wanted to save Maren, but he knew not how else but to keep her with him in the stars. Up into the air the knight threw the sword, and it did then join as one with the sky which now clapped and roared. Jorunn brought the lovers with her and Regulus, who could not live another moment without his beloved, up into a night-sky palace hidden. The four became one with the starry-dismal celestial and lived in a rare constellation surrounded by aurorean banners. Jorunn's sword had now reached its true destiny final.

On the day Modred and Arthur slew each other, a horrid silence and darkness marked the spot of their demise for three days and three nights. A permanence of desolation remained, reminding all that what good was lost and ruined here would never be emulated nor restored. People said the odd constellation hung above the grim location for those three nights and then was never again seen by any living soul. During those nights, in the feverish dreams were this story and its events seen by hermits and lovesick troubadours.

'Twas the end of the story and where Claretta, weeping, shut the book. Though touched by the tragic, I had thought, this legend was not all dismal, for the lovers of this romance had united and made their place in eternity.

IV

Nights fled, and we continued to study, catalogue, and transcribe. As I recall, the seismologists and geophysicists we were teamed up with had been rather rude and recalcitrant. Our work-relationship during this investigation with these snobby-idle churls had been fraught with quandaries because of them.

It wasn't all awful. I could always look forward to Claretta's cooking. She loved to cook for everyone, even for the scientists and volunteers. It made things a little more cheery and bright. More often, she would cook up a morningtide meal for all: drisheens, omelettes, and pancakes, all of which having been made with such a sweet and fresh-sharp taste of tansies, thyme, the sweetest of sugar, and caraway. I had always enjoyed the endearing manners she used when eating; remarkably too, she had always stayed of desirable-thin figure despite eating often.

More days passed, and many of the volunteers vanished, and most of those who remained became fatally ill. Strange hounds and wild critters came into the camp and crypt, which distressed us greatly. Time passed on, and more of the researchers were going missing. Bats plagued the laboratory and campsite. We had to hire several wildlife specialists and hunters to take care of the mangy brutes and get them out off our research area.

One morn after, Claretta, Tewodros, and I were met by the men of science. Now, of unwell countenance, they had come to our meal-table with bewildered talk of a most irregular happening. From their own atremble words, they said they'd all experienced similar nightmares the night previous, and now, just as it had foretold in the sick dreams, they were now missing a man from their erudite-lettered circle—Dr. Florimond.

Wellsprings of teary distress, a horrid sallow prowled the chilling countenances of the men of academia as they told us of their nightmares. Such hokum murmurs misbecame the self-proclaimed "science-adepts," who'd been mistreating us thus-far like we were negligible mooncalves; not a spit nor smidgen of ruth had I for them, and already my heart did case-harden. Nevertheless, still taken aback I was in a knot of goosebumps by their telling.

As they said, they dreamt bad the night previous, and their dream-visions were oddly identical. In their collective sleep-encounter saw they a spiral tunnel of spectacular size. Assailing outflows of air brought a freeze spell that did ice the veins. Beyond the tunnel were over-extensive steps, each of which must've been a chthonian eminence of rime, with each step likened to a cliff. Bizarre monuments crumbled around them. Mordant designs, which the grim compounded, dilated on the surface of these cyclopean edifices resigned to age-old isolation of immeasurable standstill.

The men spoke of a shared-intuition, a humble understanding that the implausible architecture here was somehow both frozen yet watching and animate, but not in any way similar to the machine or the plant or animal.

What I pieced out their staggering memories was that they were running and climbing downward for inestimable hours, down, and more down they sank into cosmic depth, without reaching the bottom of the gigantic stairway.

Before the dream ended, Dr. Florimond, and only he, reached the bottom. Screaming out of the subhuman black, his voice spoke of a prehistoric necropolis and its sarcophagi of astronomical and discordant proportions. He had unlocked and roused, at the center of the exceeding-ancient realm, an "unworldly machine" that began rising and pumping awful.

Florimond screeched, "The orgy of the damned! They have come! Run!"

As their waking minds took shape, and a horrible mysterious roared with avalanche power, the group heard a din like the sounds of thousands of wild animals.

I cared not for listening to any more of this hocus-pocus. They had wanted us to believe that the reason Florimond was gone was because of the dream. I didn't believe in such things of irrationality-hysteria or dream-visions. I was a man who would not be fooled by the teasing and japes of the boor. Frightened as I had been of their tale, I wasn't going to give them any more of my attention.

I hastened from that table and tried to forget them all. As I suspected, it was either they actually believed adults could share the same dream and that dreams could have consequence in the real world, or they were doing a practical joke. Magic, dreams, and monsters: all humbug, to me. Only the human senses and all that could be rationally calculated would show me what I would need to fear, not dreams or mass hysteria. Only the loving Son of God would be my judge at his time.

I had to return to my work and put the world right again. I would codify and organize the myths, legends, and folklore of the old so that the current world could see light. Yet, though I never wanted to admit it, a dubious chord in me did quiver with desire for the old pagan stories and dark dreams to be true, and thus, for my soul, I feared an obscure penalty of this slight contempt of Creation. My vocation sin-seeped, my piety would regardless keep me from perdition, I believed, and so there was no reason to linger long on shame.

After I completed my mission, I made plans to return to Tarrytown, but Claretta wanted to continue traveling with me. She said the romance-tragedy story of Sir Algautr bestirred her bosom so that she required more info on it and the book in which it was found. Her intent was for us to meet with an old woman who perchance would render us details pertaining to the crypt-volume.

I questioned her for answers, who this old woman was and how she could know anything of significance about the book. All Claretta divulged was that she had known the old woman in childhood, that the old woman had been Claretta's life-long mentor, and that they were good friends.

Claretta's smile coy and eyes come-hither—against them I could not protest, whilst ultimately she frustrated my passion, as such was her wont. A fair of mystique, her being was besotting, as was her bearing exquisite. Impelled to have her in my life, although her heart never was to beat for me, I required amity of this muse of exploration and adventure. Tewodros, feeling fluish, left us as I joined my muse, the woman who encouraged me to explore and learn new things.

We had went to Svalbard after sailing through the Arctic Ocean. She had not brought her fiancé with us, so it was only to be her and I. Unsure had I been about that detail, which did abash me guilt-ridden. Before the trip, I had pondered on if it right to take this kind of trip, alone, with a woman who was to be wed. When I had ultimately accepted, I felt queasy with indignity yet shocked with ecstatic curiosity and intensity. I delayed guilt and remorse by telling myself I would allow no adultery nor intrigue. I tried to view this as a test of mine own virtue and chivalry; not to say decadent longing for her dripping, hot thighs made no throb in my heart, but I could afford no per-manent stain of sin in my memory or on my conscience.

In Svalbard, Claretta and I had passed through breathtaking fjords and had seen gigantic firmament-rending glaciers perplexingly unfurling endlessly out from the December night and silence-beset void thereof; these limitless-looking, terrorizing surroundings did buttress and heft an ambiance of immortal dread, an imperious authority constraining aught to hushed quietness. I had still felt that same dread and eerie dominion when I stepped onto the ridged, craggy land of this Arctic region. The mountains reached off into a pitch-black infinity, so I could not see where they ended or how far up they grew, which caused a cold shudder up and down my back, for no mind was ever meant to decrypt such improbable heights. Hills towered over me. The rugged, desolate terrain spread out without end. I had never been so dwarfed or so suppressed. The shrinking moonlight revealed a perilous, inhospitable land and surrounding mountains that should not have been so extensive in all directions. A passing fog lost us our armed guard; so, lost our only protection became. Not a track of his could be followed; not a sound from him could we hear. Separated from our bodyguard, we were defenseless, for he had been the only one who had had a firearm. There was nothing to defend us from the incoming threats that could have been awaiting in the darkness above or below. Any stumble or wrong step on the dismal ice and snow could have sent us down to a crushing or impaling death! The biting wind fought against me like a thunderclap of pure pain. Dispatched were the screams of the wind, put away to moonlit stillness. This unexplainable silence penetrated my heart and threatened to separate me from all my senses, to separate me from my higher faculties of reason and self, for I could hear nothing, not even my own existence.

Cryptic nervousness crept throughout my bones, a fear that I would never learn how to reclaim my evolved, inherent cognizance from the stupefying quiet. In this area of no sound, a devolution into unhearing despair became palpable. Deaf to my thoughts and sensations, I became frozen in a weird paralysis vaguely similar to when one is in the grip of a night terror or sleep paralysis. My mind remained only with a horrific awareness that I was being ravished by an abyss and ripped away from any power to discern corruption or morality. A subconsciousness of panic and an innermost urge for life struggled against this unexpected despair. My material form had become a zombie, animalistic and languid, but I refused to surrender my will! An uncanny stirring hung about this noise-drought, a shadowy resonance my ears perceived though no sound occurred. I almost, by force of an illogical instinct, presumed there must have been a giant, unseeable something with us. My perception of this hidden ill sent a rush of fear through me, and I gained renewed strength, which I used to force out a resounding scream to free me from the hideous silence!

Claretta was screaming too, and she was looking up at the sky with arms up wide. She started speaking in a frantic jumble of unrecognizable sounds that were not words. She wouldn't listen to me, and she defied my warnings never to go far away from me. She seemed to be imploring something out there, beyond the stars. She raised up her hands and moved this way and that. I pursued her through the severe wind and dark. She was so far away from me. So distant now, she lowered herself before a grotty figure like that of a wicked beast or hunchback wretch, but I remember thinking it was vaguely like a crooked old woman.

I attempted to follow her but was covered in darkness. I pushed through and inexplicably found myself at the saw-toothed edge of a dizzying cliff. Remote mountains dared to seize the upper blackness and lick the desecrated bosom of a portentous blood moon. The enormity of this awesome world encircling me was outright prodigious; it overshadowed and devoured me, as if it was subsuming me, assimilating me into a sublime rapture commanding me to rise into vaults of unremembered dimensions or hurl myself down a deathly plummet. Storm clouds spun down with a swoop of shrieking wind thirsty for destruction and strife in the heavens. Up around the night-mantle sea of stars and nocturnal aether arose revolving thunderclouds birled and bellowing with assaulting snowfall. As much as I had feared being completely destroyed or frozen by this storm, I as well could not resist worshipping and revering this supreme wrath and testimony of almighty night, a blizzard which astounded me with curiosity and menace; I had to witness it longer, had to inhale far greater of this terrible and majestic potency of the world.

Stunned with awe, I wouldn't have seen Claretta fainted in the snow if a fleeting, shimmering swathe of moonbeams had not aimed mine eyes to her beautiful outline on the ground at the exact moment I was blown back by a painful gust. The impending snowstorm let fall fine layers of whiteness in a beginning attempt to smother her.

She seemed now awakening, a wanton serene in debauch, wrapping her nude self around a dusky shape half-hidden by a mound of snow. What hybrid something in the moonlight crouched over Claretta I did not understand. This daydream was more vivid than any musing I'd ever had before.

Removed out from my reveries, and quickened with fear of the blizzard, I trudged through the pelvis-high snow. Arrived at Claretta, I perceived she, reposed in the snow, asleep again, stripped and alone. I hastily covered her with blankets and carried Claretta off, with the idea to hide us in the first shelter I could find. Claretta had said nothing of where we were heading, and all the electronics were dead. An unseen danger gashed my leg and back. Iciness battered hostile against us whilst raw of sky and land formed to one blur. I spun to spot my enemy but saw none more than Claretta and myself. Crippled cold froze limb lame and joint stiff, and now my vision was fading too.

I felt as though the land beneath my boots were spreading out and widening, not breaking, just expanding like rubber. Dark went the lantern, reducing me to a pitch-black brushed by sick northern lights and red of moon. The snowstorm-obfuscated light only intensified the dismal nowhere and callousness of night. I was rising, and I could sense the ground below my feet was growing upward and uneasy. I slipped on ice; as I fell, I knew only that I couldn't feel Claretta in my arms any further, and I hadn't been certain if that was because she was gone or I was frostbitten; my winter gear and thermal garments failed me not, but I'd lost much energy and blood, and I passed out.

Mayhap the cold conditions upset my brain, or the fall plus mine overwhelmed emotions produced a hallucinatory impression over my memory;

nevertheless, the memory I am left with is nothing if not uncanny and unexplainable. Just before the blackout, I was almost certain, in my delirious state, that I'd espied massive, chiropteran talons flick down from the moonlight and wrench Claretta away from me. That grotesque thing, to what those talons were attached, was something I wish not to remember, a strange thing, a wrong I see only in my terrifying yet mercifully forgotten moments in nightmare. If it truly was nothing but a hallucination, then I can't be sure how my mind was ever be able to conjure such an unearthly chimera obscene.

I awoke in a hospital, and a caring, gossiping nurse explained that several scientists and other locals had found me while trying to kill a group of polar bears that had killed many. The locals had saved me by shooting the creatures that were killing their captives and were to kill me last. Imagine my horror and anguish after she said that they'd found me on a beach beside the corpses of our bodyguard, four or five townsfolk, several foreign students, a gypsy crone, Luciano, and Claretta.

It was from investigators that I learned what they thought had happened. In accord to their appraisal, the foreign students and the old woman had been wearing the skins and pelts of polar bears, disguising themselves as wild animals, and kidnapping and killing people for sacrifice-rituals at the beach, with the students under the leadership of the mysterious old woman. They must've been going on like this for many nights, and they were the ones who murdered our guard. The detectives said the people who were kidnapped were taken there for a deadly ceremony. Luciano, Claretta's betrothed, had come here looking to meet her but was also kidnapped. The locals contradict the investigators' assessment and believe the things they hunted, the things that killed townsfolk and Luciano and our bodyguard, weren't people but actual polar bears.

After finally returning to New York, I wanted to rise with contentedness to breathe in the new morns ahead, but a sinister malaise bogged me down in semi-suffocating indignation. I pressured myself to fix all my faculties and scrutiny upon my profession and responsibilities, for this was the best system to sustain a suitable veneer of soundness and to wrest me out from the mercurial tempest of testy disquietude.

No avail.

V

Months gone by—in daydreams, nightmares, and my waking-visions, I still see the Gothic crypt and dare to walk inside. There I read from the impure book metamorphosing heinous; it reveals new pages that are more ancient, pages which tell of the great machines of extraterrestrial masters and of their engines made before time, before our existence.

The book sometimes appears physically on my office table in Tarrytown, though perchance these events are mental illusions and simple madness. It matters not, for I yield to temptation, to curiosity, in my lust for the unknowable and the corrupting truth of all things, for knowledge of those supreme beings who served the greater forms that accidentally made humankind and died but will return to annihilate their creations— exactly as it says in the book. Their devices, hidden under the earth of our planet, alter the weather and open doors to other dimensions altering our own. I understand not what terrors operate the living motors of the dead rulers. Now I see where to stand in places remote to catch a glimpse of the alien race and have seen their servants as they fly across the moon. 'Tis wrote of in the book, as is information on mortal nomads who kill in honor of extraterrestrial idols.

This be not a book of false magic; 'tis a collection of science eldritch and insane engineering holding to arcane, alien laws not of our reality, of rituals that create psychic and corporeal phenomena too powerful, too terrifying for mortal brains.

I know not why the book chose me. I've tried to destroy it several times, but it escapes flame and teleports at random. Its power intoxicates the mind. I fear if one should learn how to use the alien machines, if one were to learn how use the spells of the grimoire and operate the rituals of ineffable mathematics and otherworldly geometry, which are material dangers to the soft fabric of reality, that one might only wish to hasten the apocalypse!

Forth the pages, I learned of the existence of shapeshifter beldames of half-human birth that mentor mortal women on the ancient denizens. These gypsy harridans were taught the old ways and were given the old recipes and victuals that beget disease or transformation. They indoctrinate pure human women into the far-older revering of things which survived since before primordial Man. They instruct the brainwashed females to go out when they are of marriageable age and to find one of the alien race that could accept them as a breeding mate. The more men desire her, the more she is desired by other mortal men, the more she will be found desirable by the terrible things. If the foolhardy female goeth to the location fated where demoniac doorways open, and land and sky unite, and if the entity should admit her, then intercourse will occur during a half-sleep, where the physical bodies move between worlds. Afterwards, the mortal woman must die and become her corpse a seedbed for those old unformed.

I tried to forget this nonsense, but I have heard eerie bawling out from Claretta's coffin! At night I hear inaudible cries of those incubated and stowed brood, sanguicolous growing, invisible and unseen in the maggoty womb of Claretta's corpse! I see them in dreams. At her tomb I hear them! How can I ignore aught I've learned when my anatomy doth change sanguinary? Under the light of every full moon, my bones twist more hideous. Soon, I shan't long be able to read or write or type. I must hide, must continue reading the inimical leaves, must find a reverse to my lycanthropic-transmutation that doth bathe me in blood-thirst waxing!

The End.

Black Torque Demon

I, Sir Goswin, struggled long while deciding whether to write about the macabre secrets and horrific details of my blasphemous existence. With a soul stained by hubris, I still call myself a knight. Would this terrifying story only bring unfathomable calamity and pestilence to anyone who reads it? Could its words and pages be corrupted or cursed, as I have been? Sin and wickedness have blinded me, I admit. Selfishness and pride besmirch my deeds. Madness finds those who have knowledge of my journeys, knowledge of the things I have seen, and awareness of the cruel pain that follows me. I am not worthy to ask for mercy, forgiveness, or redemption. Writing this story is only evidence of my vanity and guilt. Even if my flesh is perverse and my soul damned, I must tell this story. I must warn others of what happened to me, while there is still time for me to write of such things, while I am still sane enough to get this written. This story could be a lesson, a prophecy, for those who have fallen into mires of otherworldly labyrinths hidden beneath the dead and slain of the battlefield. It is for those who have briefly walked down unknown corridors behind reality and discovered unfathomable despair. If I am doomed to cause death and loss, then I should also use it to create some goodness and beauty among the ruins. Finally, I realized that sharing this story could bring me some comfort and healing, which I do not deserve. Mostly, I may be able to accept, with sincerity, what I now am. I realize how abhorrently selfish this may appear. I do not surrender; suicide would be a curse far more terrible. Writing about my life might keep my memories alive before I become completely inhuman and insane. Thus, I decided to write about how I became cursed to suffer and rot eternally among the dead and infernal.

The year was AD 1240. Autumn was now ending in England. I was twenty-five years old. My squire and I were traveling through a royal forest. We were granted permission to make the journey so that we could meet the innocent and noble Adelaide.

Cold and dismal was this darkening forest. A menacing, dull glow of orange light floated around us. Twilight fell upon the forest. Dark gray clouds covered the sky. All the trees appeared darker and thinner than usual. Foreboding branches curled like gnarled, boney fingers of corpses. Jagged boulders appeared much too large and misshapen. The canopy above was ragged and bleak. The foliage and underbrush were sickly and decaying. There was no snow, but the freezing air and shrieking wind were bitter.

We stopped to rest beside a moldering, faded monument depicting erst rulers and forgotten warriors of the Roman Empire. My squire Eric cleaned the horses while I tried to sleep. Our tranquility was too fleeting, for a scream flew up from some mysterious place in the shadows over yonder in the deeper, darker part of the forest. This hideous noise jolted and awoke me. The sound of this cry shocked my heart and mind with fear. Agitated and afraid, the horses then kicked, reared, and neighed in their distress.

Eric grabbed a sword and ran toward the direction of the scream. He moved into the darker shadows of the forest, despite my warning. I followed him, only to discover that he was now standing motionlessly. He gasped. I put a hand on his trembling shoulder. Panting, he bared his chattering teeth in an expression of rage and shame. His entire body was shivering.

Breathless, he looked up at me. "Alas, I am too afraid to fight what I just witnessed."

"Eric, what was it?"

"Sire, forgive me. I am a coward. I tremble with horror. Petrified, I dare not take another step lest I could lose my sanity. I saw something that has frozen my soul with horror and disgrace. It has made me immobile with disturbing fear."

"What was it, Eric?"

"It was indescribable, furious wickedness. Black robes like wings of death, unclean with blood, Sire. I, too, am unclean now simply for looking at it. I wish I could forget."

"You are too brash and foolhardy, my steadfast squire. Always, you have been too eager to prove your capabilities. You dive with mad haste into battle and look for dangerous chances to spill blood and gain glory. Eric, your thirst for adventure and your excitement has exhausted your mind."

"It was an ungodly specter, cloaked with death and dreadful darkness, Sire!"

"Eric, it was no specter or apparition, only an illusion of the forest and nightfall. You and I have been in many battles and survived many perils. Constant combat has made you excited, and you crave more for fighting. What you saw was only a trick of emotion and anticipation."

"Must I believe that you are not afraid? What was that scream? It spooked the horses."

"Eric, go keep the horses well and safe. Then, we will pray. After that, you will help me prepare. I will venture the darkness yonder, locate our mysterious traveler, and investigate the source of that cry."

I was afraid, but I could not let it control me. While Eric was taking care of the horses, I was taking care of my mind and soul. I put away my emotions and hardened my thoughts against worry or doubt. I concentrated on my trust in the wisdom of our divine savior. The goodness of this world would shield me. I believed that God would always love and protect me. At every opportunity, I would show bravery and strength, for the glory of the divine will.

After the horses were calmed, Eric and I knelt for prayer. He clasped his hands together, and I clasped mine. We whispered our prayers. I bowed my head and thought only of the power of God, our divine father, who had made everything so perfectly. Once our prayers were completed, it was time to prepare for the investigation.

Eric clothed and equipped me with my armor and weapons. My cloak, tunic, shirt, leather gloves, and trousers were black like the shadows around us. While most of my garments were black, my leather shoes were brown. A mail hood protected my head. A mail robe protected my chest, arms, torso, back, waist, and legs. The silver conical helmet I wore was decorated with ornate trefoils and floral patterns interlaced with depictions of lions and wyverns interwoven around one another. With my left hand, I used a round black shield. For weapons, I had a spear and a short sword.

After I was properly mailed and armed, I told Eric to stay with the horses and our belongings. I trod an old dirt path that led me farther into the deep, gloomy parts of the forest. I did not stop until I noticed night covering the forest. It was too difficult to see ahead. Another shriek pierced the air. Rain poured down, making the ground muddy and slippery.

Moonbeams traversed the dark, helping me see. I espied dark figures walking through a cemetery nearby. They appeared to be monks wearing black robes. Rain and darkness obscured them and their acts. I pushed away branches gripping my cloak and spear. The shadows were too deep, and the forest was much too dark here. The sounds of hissing and groans filled my ears.

As lightning charged across the sky and thunder resounded throughout the forest, I glimpsed a giant, unnatural being, which had large black wings. It must have been twelve feet tall, or more. This giant was such a grotesque and repulsive being. Its horrific form was decaying and grim.

Filled with fear, I screamed. I tried not to look at it, but panic controlled my eyes. A sinister voice inside my head told me to look; it made me look.

Black smoke and shadows surrounded the massive wings of the giant monster. Numerous glowing white human skeletons and ghostly pale shrouds of spirits were clutching these ragged leathery black wings.

Almost instantly, I knew that this creature needed to die. I had to destroy it. I followed it, but it disappeared somewhere in the night and rain.

When I arrived at the cemetery, the monks were dragging human corpses and old skeletons out of their graves and tombs. The monks reached high into the air and then threw down red lightning upon the rotting bones. Sinful animation revived the dead and transformed them into atrocious monstrosities.

Before I could attack them, I heard a voice call to me. Someone said my name. I turned around to look behind me.

A chilling, haunting voice whispered into my ears. "Beware the Vows of the Black Torque. Beware the castle of their undead knights."

I recognized this voice and to whom it belonged, yet this realization dragged me into disbelief and haunting dread. I ran to the monks. From the shadows, skeletal hands reached out and grabbed my shoulders. It was a nobleman who had grabbed me. His blue eyes were cold and eerie like the falling rain. His drawn face was white like ashes and bone. Red blood was dripping from his eyes, nose, and mouth. The blood fell onto his long white beard. A bloody laceration appeared on his throat. I attacked him but did no damage or harm, for my spear passed through the white mist of his incorporeal, ghostly body. I detected that he was not standing on the ground but floating slightly above it.

I was too terrified to think rationally. I screamed as I again attempted, in vain, to harm this phantom. "It cannot be him. He is dead. Lord Roger, it cannot be. This is ungodly. Lord Roger died several years ago. What is the apparition I see before me now? Who dares mock me with this insensitive offense against God's creation?" Fearfully, I shut my eyes as the ghost screamed and wailed.

When I opened my eyes, the night was gone. Morning had come to push away darkness and ghosts. Sunlight filled the world again. The rain was gone and the storm ended. I was sitting beside a gravestone.

"I hope that you slept well, Sire," said Eric. "Sir Goswin, you did not sleep very long. Adelaide is still praying at the grave of her father, Lord Roger, and her female attendants are beside her. Several warriors are guarding her, too."

I walked to Adelaide, hoping that the ghost of Lord Roger had not come for her. When I saw her, she was on her knees before the gravestone and burial monuments dedicated to her father. She kneeled on black silk upon the ground so that she would not sully her white dress and hose. The sunlight glistened along the fair white skin of her beautiful face. Her black veil and white wimple almost completely covered her gorgeous red hair. With an elegant voice that had a graceful intonation, she whispered to the grave. Melancholy darkened her eyes. Her exquisite lips frowned with an expression of heavy sorrow.

I felt silly for being afraid of ghosts. I knew that I was always with the grace of God. There was no need to fear nightmares. Adelaide was a good, virginal maiden. I knew that no ghost could ever harm her. She was too pure, and always had been.

After Adelaide finished her prayers, she stood up and turned to face me. "I see a spirit of hope in your green eyes, Sir Goswin."

"These eyes wish to look into yours forever. Blue and warm, your eyes are like the sky of this morning."

"When this quest is complete, my valiant knight, our eyes will look upon only the brightest mornings."

"Then, we will be forever united."

She gently laid her thin, small hand in my large, strong palm. Calmness grew within me. The soft black silk of her glove caressed the tough leather of mine. Adelaide beamed. I was smiling, too, as we looked into each other's eyes.

Adelaide was the most beautiful woman I had ever known. She was five feet tall, twenty-two years old, and her body was womanly with graceful limbs.

My friend, Sir Hugh, approached us. "Hail, friends." He then formally and respectfully bowed. "I hope that I do have permission to speak. I do not wish to interrupt anything important. When I look at you two, I see bliss and love. Always smiling to each other, always holding each other's hands when you are together, you two are inspirational. I am most glad that you have found happiness with each other. I happily anticipate your marriage. Adelaide will have a great man. Sir Goswin is six feet and three inches tall, truthful, muscular, rugged from war, and he is the strongest fighter I know."

Adelaide's expression became melancholy and gloomy again. Her wide eyes now looked downward with grief. "My uncle will not allow me to be married to Sir Goswin until after we have completed our mission." Her voice was now almost a whisper. Her beauty and sadness haunted me. Even though she appeared so unhappy, her face was still elegant and refined. "We must end my family's curse."

"I still do not understand it," said Sir Hugh. "Adelaide's uncle is a wise and wealthy baron. Now, he wants her to go to a castle to help poor and sick people so that she can stop a family curse? How can the baron believe all this?"

I said, "Edmund believes that his family has been cursed now for one hundred years. He thinks if we do an act of great kindness, we can destroy the evil that is haunting his family."

"I am happy to go to the castle of the Black Torque Knights," said Adelaide. "I want to bring faith and kindness to those who are suffering. The Vows of the Black Torque is a chivalrous and knightly order. Those knights and monks are giving shelter and medicine to lepers, pilgrims, and wounded vagrants infected with disease. I will pray with them, wash the unclean, feed the hungry, and show the dying the light of our savior so that they may remember God and find salvation."

After hearing Adelaide speak of the Vows of the Black Torque, I remembered my nightmare. I remembered her father, Lord Roger. His warning reverberated in my mind. I was cold, and my chest felt tight. Worry was squeezing me.

I looked at Sir Hugh. "You do not believe that curses are real?"

Sir Hugh derisively waved his hand, scoffingly puffed, and then snorted with contempt. "I believe only in God. I fear only God. Faith and strength will bring peace. Whatever may be the outcome or consequence, I will do anything I can to protect you on the journey. Curses and ghosts could never be real in this world, because our heavenly father created everything perfectly."

I did not want to dishearten Adelaide by talking more about the tragedies that had befallen her family and killed many of her relatives. Hugh was certainly not willing to talk more about it. He did not believe in curses or magic. Adelaide had already been suffering and mourning for many years. She had witnessed misfortunes and disasters that destroyed the lives of her grandparents, cousins, and others related to her family's bloodlines. When her mother and father had died, mystery and paranoia had surrounded the strange circumstances of their gruesome deaths. Gossip and outrage followed. Adelaide had been grieving for the diseases, miscarriages, mutilations, betrayals, and conflicts that ruined all sides of her family.

I understood why her uncle, Edmund, would think that there was a curse. I did not blame him for wanting to take actions against his perceived doom. I believed that he was worried for the lives of his daughter and niece. Adelaide had no other family. She was living with Edmund and his daughter Hildegard. I was not sure what to believe. I did not want to keep talking about it here. I did not want to continue thinking about it.

Images and sounds from my nightmare came back to me. I did not want to worry. I could never show fear. Adelaide needed my strength and courage, not my doubts or superstitions. I felt sinful for even giving these fearful thoughts power over my attention. I needed to focus on the goal. I needed to help Adelaide get to the castle of the knights who belonged to the Vows of the Black Torque. I would help her give aid and faith to the poor and sick who were being treated in this castle. After that, we could return home, and then Adelaide and I could finally be married, with Edmund's approval. That was the plan.

At the start of the afternoon, we continued our travel to the castle. We had servants, goats, horses, carts, and wagons coming with us. We journeyed alongside pilgrims, warriors, nuns, and priests. The warriors were all brave men from nearby territories of Edmund's barony and domains. The pilgrims, priests, and nuns had come to join Adelaide and offer their aid for the sick and dying in the castle. Several knights and their squires also joined us. My squire was beside me. Adelaide was riding beside her female attendants.

As dusk swept in, we entered an uncanny, murky woodland. Billowing pale fog covered the brutish path. Whistling wind blew against us. White mist drifted above and all around. Every branch looked like skeletal black hands reaching across the moonlight. The figures of each tree resembled shadowy warriors that were once men and now returned from cold graves. The underbrush and vegetation here was increasingly becoming more tangled and freakish, growing unnatural thorns, sharp leaves, and lumps.

Adelaide's female attendants shrieked and wailed with fear. Some pilgrims, and even some of the warriors, were now whispering things about pagan superstitions.

"This is a haunted wood filled with monsters and the evil spirits of things from times before humankind existed," said a servant. Terror squeezed her voice. She flinched and gasped as she was anxiously turning her head. She kept her trembling hands up near her face to obscure the sight of frightening things. Her wide, frantic eyes were peering all around.

Father Otto grimaced at this ranting woman. "Keep still your blasphemous tongue, you hysterical hag, and repent with prayer! Speak not of unholy beings, sinful wench. Only fear God!"

A pilgrim screamed and a warrior attacked something among the trees. Out of the fog and shadows jumped a gang of bandits, furiously yelling. Blades clashed against shields in the darkness. Spears, dripping with blood, tore through throats. Screams and shouts clawed the air of this cold night. Blood, fresh and hot, dripped off the gnarled branches above.

The bandits killed many of our warriors. The strength and courage of the knights thwarted our enemies' efforts to take prisoners. With a sharp sword, I chopped off the heads and arms of any carrying away a pilgrim or slave into the night. My blade disemboweled those bandits who tried to rob away our supplies or to steal the women.

Adelaide was sobbing. "Please, spare their lives! Prithee, show mercy! Too foul is this fight!" Her voice was pained and forlorn yet still melodious and enchanting.

Fog rolled over dozens of corpses, friends and foes, that had fallen and were now sprawled and strewn upon the path. A rancid stench of blood crawled onto my senses. The bandits were now all defeated, but one. To honor the earnest request of Adelaide, I commanded the surviving warriors and knights to allow him to live. We took him as a prisoner and brought him with us.

After enduring a harsh thrashing, the prisoner said, "Pray ye, honorable knights, stop torturing me. I will tell you everything. You may call me Guillaume. I am a knight, too. I follow the command of my masters. I have orders, from the Vows of the Black Torque, to pillage the nearby areas and rob anyone who comes along these woodland paths. My fellow knights, chevaliers, and I use the plundering to gain wealth and resources for the knightly leaders who command the Vows of the Black Torque. Return me to their castle, which resides on a desolate moor. I am certain that they would pay for my return. The ransom would be generous and greatly beneficial, so you must keep me alive and safe. I warn you now; cursed are these haunted lands. We should not stay here for long."

Adelaide said, "The Vows of the Black Torque is a virtuous and chivalrous order of knights. You conjure falsehoods. They would never order anyone to cause pillage, murder, robbery, and plunder only for wealth and power. They heal sick people, they give food to the hungry, and they give shelter to the homeless. What you say must be a trick. Please, I ask only for honesty."

Guillaume laughed bitterly and loudly. Sir Hugh shouted at him and then bludgeoned him repeatedly. Blood poured out of Guillaume's nose and lips, making his bloody smirk a revolting expression of mockery. After binding and shackling Guillaume, we wrapped ropes around his arms and torso and then tied him to a knight's horse.

We continued onward, moving closer and closer to the castle of the Vows of the Black Torque. We moved through a dark dale, traversed a barren heath, and passed a gloomy down and eerie tors. When we reached the moor, nighttime was still shrouding the sky in blackness.

I feared that this darkness would never end. I wanted to see sunlight, not shadows or moonlight. We had traveled a long time, and I could not stop myself from wondering if the morning was being kept hidden away from us.

The moor was a rocky, desolate place. Bitter wind swooped in and howled. Adelaide, Hugh, the other knights, Father Otto, Sister Marjorie, and I rode across the decaying landscape. Our horses moved carefully and slowly. Guillaume hobbled and staggered as his captor's horse pulled him. The servants, pilgrims, warriors, the other remaining priests and nuns, the female attendants, and the squires all marched behind us.

As we traveled on the moor, I felt so small. I pondered whether we were actually crawling across a threatening abyss that was expanding. There was even something unsettling about the moonbeams that fell on us and followed our movements. Yawning, groaning wind returned. The moor now appeared more like a primeval, brutal place shrouded with blackness. The grass and other vegetation seemed dead and old.

The rocky landscape of the moor seemed too weird and unnatural. It was as if this was a barren, lonely place ripped open by the colossal claws and diabolic hands of unfathomable, evil things. Maddening was the wailing wind and every sobbing breeze, which disoriented and unnerved me. My heart was pounding against my ribs. I wanted to get to the castle before the winds and darkness of the moor completely blasted away my mind.

I feared that I might become invisible or evaporate. Yet, there was some mysterious beauty here, a seductive element, which intrigued and enthralled me. I could not understand what I was feeling or from where these thoughts were coming. I felt as if I was close to something truly honest but damning.

Shame and feelings of wickedness gripped my mind. As my breathing was getting more heavy and raspy, I thought I heard the cries and screams of those bandits whom I killed in the wood. As much as it spooked me to hear them, I enjoyed their terror. A slight smile manifested like a ghost on my lips.

When we finally arrived at the decrepit castle, a strange monk opened the doors and allowed us to enter. He did not speak much, and the expression of his gaunt face seemed more like a constant scowl. When asked for his name, he only said that he was Brother Miodrag. Trying to get any other information from him was exhausting and confusing. He was incredibly stubborn and apathetic. I asked him to give us information about Guillaume, the knights of this castle, and Adelaide's mission. Miodrag gave us nothing but silence or gibberish. We asked him where the other monks and knights were. Miodrag said they were here but not where we could see them. We asked him to bring us to the sick and hungry who needed our help. Miodrag ignored those questions and then walked away.

The walls of the castle were cracked and decaying. Cobwebs and dust lingered on the broken furniture and clung to the windows. I commanded the servants to start making more illumination. This place needed more candlelight, so I had them light candles for us to see clearly enough. Some servants lit torches while others cared for our horses and supplies. Eric and the servants went outside to put the horses and Guillaume in the stables.

Several minutes passed. Someone was pounding on the doors and screaming from outside the castle. Recognizing the voice, I knew that it was Eric. He had returned. I opened the doors and saw him covered with bleeding wounds. He stumbled and gripped my arm.

"Guillaume is free," said Eric. He gasped and coughed blood. "All the servants are dead. It happened in the stables. I was going to keep Guillaume locked in there with the horses. The servants started falling. Guillaume killed the horses. He attacked me. I stabbed him, my sire. I know my blade hit him, but he still escaped and ran away. I thought he was coming for you next. I am glad that you are safe." Eric's eyes closed.

I laid Eric's corpse on the floor and whispered prayers for his eternal rest. Adelaide wept when she realized that Eric had died. The female attendants cried and moaned with grief. The pilgrims screamed and begged for mercy. The priests and nuns somberly prayed for Eric's soul.

We were all going to leave this doleful castle and take Eric's corpse with us, but the doors would not open. Darkness filled the castle. Filling the room, an odorous wind gasped and lunged from out of the shadows. All the candlelight died, taken by this repugnant wind. We were trapped inside. The warriors and knights attempted to break down the doors and windows, but they could not do damage.

Shocking, dreadful screeches penetrated the darkness and horrified me. The attendants and pilgrims cried and screamed with terror. Droves of humanoid enemies, each was wearing black robes, ran out of the passageways and circled us. The sounds of swords and knives slicing and stabbing through human flesh oozed loudly across the shadows. The noises of cracking bones and gushing blood flooded my senses. Only moonlight traversing the cobwebbed lancet windows revealed vague outlines and delusive images of the almost inexplicable, dreadful battle that now befell us all with turmoil and brutality in the shadows. The ogees of the windows dripped blood as our warriors were haled and thrown up into the air.

The grunting monks slammed against our shields. These foes attempted to grab and throw us. I foined and sliced at any enemy coming too close to Adelaide or me. I bashed the skulls of the hissing monks with my shield. Some squires finally lit several more torches, filling the room with needed illumination.

The orange glow chewed through the shadows, and revealed the frightening faces of our enemies. Before, I had presumed that these monks were human. Now, because of the torch flames, I realized that these enemies were comprised of supernatural villainy and shocking horridness. I supposed that these were devilish creatures pretending to be human monks. Perhaps they were things that worshipped some manner of mockery against human design. I did not want to believe what I was seeing. I wanted to prevent the knowledge of these monsters from entering my memory and corrupting my soul.

These monks had human bodies, yet still inhuman were their necks, faces, and heads. Each had the face of a large black spider with soulless red eyes. They had twisted horns on the top of their skulls. Dozens of reptilian eyes were connected to the many tentacles protruding from their heads. At the front of their faces were long black fangs. They had snake tongues flicking out their mouths. Wide black fins were attached to their serpentine, elongated necks; these fins had many eyes on them, too.

The poison breath and fangs of the monks defeated the strong knights and brave warriors. The monks ripped apart our soldiers and used the corpses as weapons. The squires were quickly slaughtered.

More blood dripped from the walls. Bodies slammed to the floor. Sir Hugh and I continued fighting the monsters. We used our shields to protect us from the venomous spray. He and I chopped off heads and arms of these abhorrent things until all were slain.

Sister Marjorie grabbed my hand and gave me a torch. She was weeping and trembling. "Guillaume captured Adelaide! He took her deeper into the castle!"

Sir Hugh screamed and stabbed a monk's corpse. "This is impossible. Adelaide is a fair, beautiful, and chaste damsel. She is pure and good. Those devils should not exist. How have those things taken her? How did all our soldiers fall so easily?"

I said, "I wish this were only a nightmare. How could I let this happen? Sir Hugh, Father Otto, Sister Marjorie, please forgive me for being weak. Now, we are the only survivors; we are all that is left, but we can still rescue Adelaide. Father Otto and Sister Marjorie, please, bless all our weapons and armor so that we may vanquish the incarnate evil that lives in this castle."

Father Otto and Sister Marjorie silently prayed. Then, they put their hands on our weapons and armor; asked God for mercy and divine strength; and finally, they begged for forgiveness.

Father Otto looked up to the rib vault ceiling. "Let the intentions of our holy father hold to these spears and swords."

Sister Marjorie put her head to the floor. "Let the most divine voice and righteous might manifest upon the shields and armor of these brave knights."

It was now time to rescue Adelaide. As we walked through the labyrinthine stone passageways of the castle, we walked under Gothic arches and passed many grotesques on the walls. Father Otto and Sister Marjorie carried the torches so that Sir Hugh and I could be more ready to fight.

As we walked up a sinuous stairway, horrid spectres ambushed us. They brandished their spears as they floated behind and before us. These ghosts looked like the living corpses of dead men wearing torn cloaks and ragged clothes. Their garments and flesh were made of glowing white mist and pale sparks. Their eyes were wisps of green flames.

Sister Marjorie fell down through a trapdoor and disappeared in the darkness below. Father Otto had tried to grab her hand, but he was too slow. With our weapons glowing with white light, Sir Hugh and I smote the ghosts. Guillaume was at the top of the staircase. He had a knife pressed against the white luminous skin of Adelaide's neck.

Moonlight glistened on Guillaume's blade and the silver circlet around Adelaide's head. Her long straight red hair was billowing with the sudden breeze. Red blood dripped down her white shoes and white hose. Guillaume laughed, and Adelaide begged him for mercy. When I ran to them, they disappeared.

Miodrag jumped down and pierced Sir Hugh's chest with a spear. Miodrag cackled and then pointed at me. "The masters will destroy your soul, Sir Goswin! You will die here, too, like your friends! We will burn your soft white skin. We will cut off your long light brown hair. We will stab your green eyes! You will boil! Your memories will provide succor for the masters! Your bones will become dust!"

Miodrag attacked, but I dodged and stabbed him through the eyes. A mysterious door opened out of the wall; Guillaume ran out of the doorway and attacked, but I blocked with my shield. Miodrag's corpse rolled down the stairs. Guillaume now appeared like a walking, decaying zombie. Dozens of ghouls, revenants, and crawling human skeletons joined him.

Father Otto was not strong enough to push away the swarm of undead foes. Skeletal, rotting hands ripped open his face. Bloody teeth tore his heart out of his chest. I had tried to save him. I had been cutting and striking against the hungry corpses and ghouls, but there were too many of them, and I did not reach Otto fast enough. I did not allow any of these enemies to survive and destroyed them all with my spear. A furious yell thundered from me, and my weapon cut off Guillaume's head.

Now, I was all alone. The monsters killed everyone else. No, Adelaide was still alive. She was still being kept somewhere in this perplexing castle. I could not lose hope. I would rescue this damsel. The fight was not yet over. Thinking about her rescue and safety, I dashed through macabre hallways that were dripping blood and filled with lumbering ghouls eating human corpses. I entered decaying vaults in which the dead were rising. Stone grotesques walked off the broken walls and attacked me. While I was destroying all these monsters, I always was thinking of her.

Finally, I reached a wide underground hall. Candles threw soft light into this dark, haunting room. The floor was covered with bones, some of which were human and some animal. I saw Adelaide's slender, womanly body on the floor. I ran to her and noticed that she was still alive and unharmed. Her white dress was torn, but she had no wounds.

I cut the ropes restraining her. She hugged me as I was looking around the room to make sure that she was safe. I heard something move behind us. I spun and used my shield to block a dagger aimed for my back, thwarting the enemy's cowardly attack. Turning my head, I saw no enemy. I walked around the room, but knew not whence the dagger came.

Out of the darkness walked a hellish foe. This man was maybe eight or nine feet tall. Black, heavy mail covered his entire body. His mail hood revealed his grim face, which was rotting and cadaverous. He had no eyes, nose, or lips. His hands were long and gnarled. His sharp bloody claws tore out of his ragged mail gloves. He stood tall and straight. He was bedighted with black garments and armor. His torn surcoat was completely black and covered with cobwebs. His mail boots dripped blood and dirt.

He swept toward me and pounded my shield with phenomenally vicious blows from his red sword. His awing puissance broke my spear and shattered my shield. I pulled out my sword and attacked, but he was far swifter. After he dodged my attack, his blade cut open my left arm. The pain was so dreadful

I screamed and could only concentrate on the cold malice of this torment. The agony in my arm soared all throughout my entire body like a winter storm.

When the undead knight again attacked, I could not move. The freezing pain immobilized me. The blade pierced my torso. The horrid enemy grabbed my throat with a cold hand. I was utterly stunned from the intense feelings of pain shocking my mind and body. I felt his rancid breath blow out of his open mouth.

A low, dreadful voice slowly drifted out of his bleeding skull. This undead knight's empty eye sockets began to burn with red flames. "I, Sir Dragomir, offer this knight to the torque. With bracing blood and black wind, the advent of our demon master finally betides. Edmund gave us Adelaide as a sacrifice to end the curse I had put on his family one hundred years ago. Edmund's ancestors had stolen the torque from us, but now all will be corrected. When the torque returns, the curse will be lifted, after the death of Adelaide. For his strength and prowess, I have chosen Goswin to become our newest member, a demon of the torque."

Hildegard, the seductive and sinful daughter of Edmund, sauntered into the room. A vain expression lingered on her calculating eyes. Her white skin seemed vaguely to be glowing pale light in the darkness. Light from her candle glistened against her long straight black hair.

Edmund arrived, too. Dark blemishes were around his sunken eyes. He appeared mysterious and morose. His white skin was sickly and pallid. As he scowled, his frown was narrow, and his mouth hung slightly open, revealing his sharp teeth. His heavy breathing was loud. His claws clenched a black armband, which he now obediently gave to Dragomir. Adelaide screamed when she saw Hildegard, brandishing a knife, coming closer toward her. Adelaide ran towards me, but Hildegard stabbed her through the back.

Adelaide's dying words were, "Let the dolor of this night and my death bring purity. Goswin, take my purest feelings. I will always be praying for you. Save our souls. We will always be together, Goswin. I shall never leave your soul."

Adelaide's corpse sank to the floor, but my body began glowing with brilliant white light. I pushed away Dragomir and grabbed Hildegard's blade. I decapitated her and Edmund, swiftly. Dragomir hissed and screeched, seemingly afraid of the glowing light around me. I vanquished Dragomir with my weapon and stabbed his body until he was only icy dust. The glowing light vanished.

I must have sat beside Adelaide's corpse for hours. I wailed and screamed, still holding her slender body. I cried alone, praying that she would return to life. Furious, I finally stood and held my weapon up high above my head. I attacked the armband that was resting in the frozen dust of Dragomir's corpse. I just wanted to attack something to release my fury.

A loathsome voice echoed in my mind, telling me to attack the armband. My rage consumed my thoughts until I willfully abandoned all reason and rationality. I wanted anger to control my acts. I wanted to hone my flesh for hatred against the torque that had been at the center of so many deaths and frightening phenomena.

Exactly as my blade hit the torque, a sound clambered into my ears. A nightmarish, hellish voice manifested. "My new devilish servant!"

My blade shattered, unable to damage the black torque. From out the morbid armband, black clouds and white lightning now jumped. The clouds brought a storm that destroyed the castle. I shut my eyes and felt the falling stones and crumbling walls crush me.

Reanimated, I awoke and beheld the giant man from my nightmare. He must have been more than twelve feet tall. He had goatish black horns growing from his white boney head. His grim face was decaying and skeletal. Long black hair hung from his head. His white tail was long and slimy. He had a snake tongue, black ragged wings dripping black filth, and he wore a black robe.

The giant said, "Goswin, I have waited for you. Wear my torque, and conquer the wintry battlefields. Rise with my undead knights, and spread death."

I lost faith and devotion to all my old beliefs. The sight of this giant corrupted my soul. My dejection and madness brought me to a dizzy world of ghosts and shadows. Bloodlust and feverish barbarity spread throughout my flesh and brain. Seduced and horrified, I took the torque. I tried to resist, but I wanted power and feared everything. I was a servant left only with dreadful insanity. My rage and horror consumed me. The more I tried to fight it, the greater the anxiety became.

Every winter, I have risen with Dragomir and his warriors. We are doomed eternally to wander battlefields, kill, and then die again at spring. The year now is AD 1840. Many languages have I learned. Often, I am too insane to remember anything. Sometimes, I feel Adelaide holding me and praying for my salvation. I have only damned her soul, and she is forever imprisoned in the shadows around me.

Hatred and loneliness have pushed me aside into a paradoxical wasteland that is older than reality. There are dark places beyond the world of gods and mortals. In these places, there are unknowable, horrifying entities that twist minds and open up unfathomable realms of deep despair. These morbid beings carry the homes of otherworldly magic that have always been here. They are soulless and apathetic towards humanity. Their existence effortlessly distorts reality and dreams. Howbeit, I walked into this abyss and found great beauty in the danger and bloodshed.

Now, I must rest in my tomb. I will rise next winter. I fight to keep the fear away. It is all I can do. The glory and thrill of combat is all I have left to hold together my ghostly sanity. Every year, I become increasingly more and more inhuman. Maybe, one day, I might look upon this and give a dry laugh. I might one day remember the humanity I had left and then completely die in the filth and slime of this haunted world. I can hear the din of the demons and giants. Adelaide's singing keeps me from complete oblivion. Perhaps, one might say that all of this was to preserve our love.

The End.

Dubhdris Abbey

Prologue

Rumors of unfamiliar wildlife, of things that should not be, appearing in the Adirondack Mountains have been spreading over the last few years, especially so among those who have done much hiking or camping there. Some have even whispered, though always behind locked doors and closed windows, of the doglike salamanders or wolfish anthropoids that have stalked them while in the wilderness stretching across those mountains whose bogs, under eeriest Samhain moon, do release mossy, fungous heaps of the most rancid and debased hybrid forms of frogs, snakes, bats, vermin, coyotes, and spiders—all of which do leap and dance and copulate intermingled until dawn, all of them breeding with one another in ways that should not be possible between so many different types of amphibians and reptiles and mammals and bugs, like an absurd Walpurgis Night orgy of frenzy and revelry.

There are those who remember the mysterious Italian monk "Fra Italo", whose gelatinous corpse was discovered in one of those bogs, and whose legs showed a type of damage not much different from vaporization or disintegration; and just as strange about Fra Italo is that he was seen in a monastery in Catanzaro of Italy just one day before he was found dead in New York of the United States.

Folk-legend tells of the terrible monks—Brother Hipolit, Brother Omar, Brother Bartel—who were caught on the Adirondack Mountains making child-sacrifices to the callous, ancient blood-chiefs, sometimes known as the "Grumocruths," of the eldritch swamp. What happened to the three monks is still a mystery. It is also said that Brother Franco of Dubhdris Abbey took his life after he learned the truth of their ceremonies. Others say Brother Franco is still alive, but not in any human goings; they say he runs wild with the dogs of the mountains and joins them in orgiastic ritual and black delight.

Many still deny all the rumors, but even some of who do will tell they have heard of the young men who went missing and the group who went out to rescue them. They might reveal they've seen black cloaks scudding up the mountains and disappearing without trace.

Uncorroborated folklore of the region tells us a group of survivalists and environmentalists discovered a portal into the northmost portion of the Adirondack Mountains; these men entered the opening unknown but got trapped within a labyrinth in which they wandered for five days before finally finding themselves in an underground Gothic crypt. Once there, a plaque on the wall read "Dubhdris Abbey. Tarrytown. New York." Under a pile of bones was a fetid parchment-like manuscript: "The Last Words Of Guerino Fusco". The group said that they carried it off with them while they were under assault of some unknowable beast. What chased the men out of the crypt was a horror too difficult to explain, too hideous to describe. Each of the men gave different descriptions of the unnamable item of pure insanity, but what they could agree on was that there were parts of the gigantic creature that seemed like a wolf with sharp teeth, and yet it had fleshy tendrils and many, many arms, misshapen limbs, and extensive tentacles; it was a thing part-arachnid, part-dog, and simian-like, but it moved as if it was only an attachment to something far more nebulous and shapeless in the dark. The horror pursued them back throughout the labyrinth, and the group only escaped by jumping through a webby chasm and exiting into the Hudson River. The men sent the manuscript to be passed around.

This is what the manuscript says:—

The Last Words Of Guerino Fusco

In an old, mouldered chamber of a tavern in Killarney, a mighty beautiful spot of dear Ireland, I was enjoying my late-evening beer when I heard my name whispered by a voice familiar, one I hadn't heard in so, so long. I turned round and discovered it was only me in this small room; well, that's what I thought until eventually discerning, to my chagrin and trepidation, a soiled hand or claw of something in a distorted, dark corner of the chamber. Then from shade there emerged an eldritch outline of something wrong, obscure. It progressed near my only exit, so I dared not move. As it got closer, I perceived it held a similarity to a man whom I hadn't seen in almost ten years, an old friend named Rutger who had once been long-familiar in my more halcyon days. As the prowler drew nearer, and it gave me a better look of itself, I decided it might be a man as I'd thought, but I still didn't think for certain whether or not it were my old pal; this guy seemed so much more pallid and gaunter and more tense than how my friend had been the last time I'd seen him.

Rutger had always been a well-off man of perfect etiquette; he had always been a warm and friendly gentleman, and I'd always known him to be prim and polished anywhere he went. Rutger had enjoyed long conversations, polite discourse, and he had been chatty; one of his favorite pastimes was gossip and gossiping with unknown persons; so, as he would say it, he needed to be "presentable and benign," and this had worked for him, allowed him to make friends very easily. Many people, from many different culture-circles, had thought of him as a trustworthy and harmless sort. He had loved to dress with bright color and total sophistication. That was the Rutger I knew.

What stood before me now in the growing darkness was a being all dressed in black, dirty rags; his black hair was a wild mess; he smelled of disgusting decay and all the putrescence of the dead; dirt and grime still clung to his naked toes and fingers; his skin was somber white like dusty bones; and that skin of his seemed too tight.

Indeed, the immediate appearance of this blighter actually gave me shivers upon first glance, like he were a pale limb of spooky shadow loomed forth the darkness as night sharpened its claws against the sky corroding visible through the pointed-arch window. Like some alert owl, his eyes widened disk-like, and his leer became a fearful stare, like a frightened animal or anxious predator. Stiff and straight down against his sides hung the long, rigid arms of this male form whose bizarre, unsettling mien was like that of an eerie miscreant. He even stood upright and firm with unnatural stillness and artificial posture. A grimace twitched at his face. Aspects of the crooked frown, heavy breathing, and partly open mouth of this visitor whispered of an encumbrance and strain from which he could not be rid.

Fear had spoilt my sight then, I should assume; for a second, I almost thought that in some peculiar way, like floating, not walking, the menacing creep was inching closer to me. I still don't know how he did it: he advanced silently, maybe motionless in a way that shouldn't be possible. It made my head hurt looking at him. His feet touched the floor, like normal, but his legs moved not; with silence was he drifting or sliding, and the only sounds in the room were his long breaths.

The memory of this is confused and disarranged by time and many night-mares, so I'm sure I'm not remembering what happened correctly. That's what I'd like to assume, but you never know with these things, these horrible visions that creep into the mind up from some unknown gulf of madness and loneliness.

I do remember how a terror-struck gasp escaped my mouth then, and I jumped back from the stranger. I would have ran, but I became paralyzed in part by horror and partly by a hypnotic curiosity and desire for knowledge; I almost couldn't look away from this awful fellow who was subverting my understanding of normalcy and reason, someone who defied everything I thought a human could look like or should. Much too unnatural. I couldn't move my feet in this fear.

The face of this unknown person especially reminded me so much of my friend Rutger's. I can't explain it. Yet this new man was so dissimilar from the old Rutger, a man I would have been happy to see and talk with. I yearned to reacquaint myself with my old friend, and that need made me want to risk danger to collect information right from this threat, someone who looked like Rutger, even if the similarity was only slight.

I tried to think of what to do, tried to move, tried to think reasonable. I didn't want this thing attacking me. I was almost certain that what was approaching was a petrifying parody, a shabby doppelganger of Rutger; however, a nagging suspicion screamed in my bosom that this was my friend Rutger and that I should commune with this irrational force from the past, one who was once my friend. I think his hands were beginning to move up toward me.

I forced myself to speak over the panic and said to him, "Uh—Rutger? Rutger, is it really you, ol' chap?"

The unpleasant counterpart recoiled and became twitchy, looking behind his shoulders, looking out the window. Then, his hands lowering gently, this demented excuse for a man quieted his breathing. His eyes squinted and looked into mine. He may have been studying me. After what felt like an unbearable length of time and silence, the man spoke, and his voice was hoarse but surely recognizable as the voice of my old chum.

"Aye. Be it me, Guerino. Mo chara. 'Tis Rutger, yer ol' mate."

Moving just a slight to the door, I never took my eyes off him. To run or to stay: I was torn between the hooks of horror and the lure of the irrational. I knew not how to feel that this deviant knew my first name, too.

I wanted to scream, but, fearing how that would make him react, I willed a scrap of self-control.

Instead, I said, "Umm. Well. Where'd ya just come from—sneakin' all 'round the place, were ya?"

The man said no normal reply, but he startled me with a loud grunt, and he wheezed gross. Now I could barely speak with my lips aquiver. I started toward him, to see if he were really Rutger. I didn't know what to say to him; I didn't want to anger him into attacking me; I was deeply confused. If he were my friend, he wouldn't want to scare me so, I thought.

Another idea jumped through my brain: I anticipated that if I didn't say something anon, he would be irritated and attack anyway.

"You've startled me something mighty horrified," I said, trying hard not to stutter. "I don't know what you're doing here. Are you all right? Has something happened to you?"

"The Abbott and his monks are waiting and have sent me to remind you," he said. "Be not afraid to join us."

"Do I know you? What is this? Please, explain yourself, or I'll alert the police!"

His response, in that low voice, breathy and ominous, like a grim rush, now carried an ancient property most morbid and bleak, an almost-guttural and sometimes-whistling up and down of speech, which I'd never heard any human voice express. It certainly didn't sound like Rutger any longer. He spake of family leaders, more-wickeder illusions, hidden flesh, and a number of strange unfamiliars that did cold my blood affright.

"Wirra!" He said. "A thou-times—Aye, Guerino, Aye, 'tis me in sooth. Run not me away from! I was yer friend Rutger, and he am I, still. Anon, like me shalt thou be! If thou wouldst only encalm, prithee. Hark! Thee take will Dubhdris Abbey. Thou art for thy sooth famigliarch needed. Be it ancient inheritance ours. Art thou old 'nough and thy metafeoil finally ready aneath thine innards. Lo na neromealltach nightmares, them black gulfs folding deceit by dimensions shift round—as the bloodthirst enquickens!"

I ran out the chamber and back into my private room, the one I'd paid for, which was in this same tavern. I locked the door and got the phone but dropped it from trembling hands.

Dizzy and frantic, fear preventing me from using my voice, not knowing if I would ever speak or even breathe again, I stumbled across the floor; and what happened next was I must've been so scared that I passed out on the settee and had a horrid absorption of dreaming; for, what happened in my private room after I dropped the phone was something that defies any convention.

I can only hope it was a dream; for the sake of candor and sharing in full, I'll relate all occurrences to the best of my ability, in the correct sequence of such events as I believe they took place. If it was not a dream, if it was not a passing sickness of my mind, then what we have is something far more troubling that needs to be exposed, so all must need to know that such things, things which we've all been taught are false, are real.

As I remember, from where the dream might have begun, a nauseous smell acetic and mephitic upset my living-space. I needed air in this stuffy room, so I opened a few windows. The wind whistled, and I was reminded of the chilling voice of Rutger, like I could still hear him speaking to me. Autumn moonbeams radiant through the lancet windows, the chamber took on a lunar-blue tone, which I had never seen before, had never seen the moonlight become so blue.

Then the howls and cries of what could have been wolves pierced the black vault above the moon, their echoes floating, decaying into the unknowable nowhere and unimaginable beyond of night; so loud was it all that I could hear it in my room as if a pack of wolves were right on top of me.

Multitudes of dark shapes rushed through the open windows. Flittering about the room, these intruders screeched and squeaked. Circling my head, these raucous fliers clicked and chirped as I swatted at them. I could only guess that these were bats; stranger was they appeared too abnormal for this region: they were large, plump, black, and seemed to be over-sized kin to vampire bats!

A horrible scratching noise, as if a large number of talons were climbing on the walls from outside, like living things were actually crawling up and down the full exterior of the tavern. Vast buzzing intruded into the roaring mayhem. What appeared to be swarms of locusts entered from beneath the cracks and gaps of the broken floorboards. Muddy abnormalities seized my room with filthy noise: belching toads, nasty grasshoppers, chirping crickets, trilling katydids, and hissing vipers; all were malformed and did not at all appear to belong to this land.

At the same moment I reached for the doorknob, the maddening cacophony growing, the door creaked open slightly. I screamed for help, not wanting to go near the door but not wanting to stay here. Bugs poured out the keyhole. Something was moving out from the gap between the ajar door and the wall. I yelled for the tavern innkeeper. A malicious sniggering leapt from yonder darkness beyond the open windows. The taunting laughter pounded my bosom with terror as a pale claw emerged from behind the door and clutched its wooden frame, leaving an oozing slime to drip like blood and stain red the floor in spots and horrid clumps. I must have been bitten by hungry pests and lost a lot of blood, which might account for my hallucinations; for next I saw a horrid and indescribable monster so nightmarish and against all human thought that I fainted.

My mind won't even let me recall many details of what I'd seen of the nightmare-thing; all I can say is that I think it was guzzling, wolfing down its victims—the being using its numerous fleshy tendrils and many hands and a large number of limbs and paws and many other appendages, if that was what they were, appendages that were too hard to describe and were all attached to this sinewy monstrosity—flaying or feasting on the innkeeper and several others before my loss of consciousness. That dream becomes more fuzzy and nebulous still, more abstract, the more I think about it, the more time that passes.

Anyway, after fainting, I jolted upright from the settee and screamed awake out of the nightmare. Quiet was the daybreak. Chill came the October air. It was like no time had passed at all from night to morning. Dawn broke through the windows. Large leaves covered the interior of my chambers. They must've blown in from all the open windows, presumably. Even I was covered in a pile of the red, green, black, purple, brown, and yellow of them all. The floor was soaking wet as the ceiling dripped down upon me. Profuse amounts of twigs were on the floor too. A tree had fallen and broken through one of the windows, must've happened while I was out cold; one of its branches kept its gnarled clutch around my neck.

At that time, I believed that everything from the night previous had been a dream gone bad, that I'd been drinking too much and was on too much medication all the while. That's why I didn't call the police that day. I told myself monsters could never be real and those animals and bugs could never be here. I assumed I'd never actually seen Rutger and the experiences from last night were brought on by intoxication and bad weather. Everyone sane knew there were no ghosts or demons or monsters or aliens in our reality. Everyone knew animals and bugs could never behave like they had in my dream, they could never act with such intelligent malevolence and destructive purpose. It just wasn't common, wasn't known. I'd never heard of animals attacking in such great numbers while swarming into a room with so many other different types of beasties outside their own species. If I had told anyone about all these events, they'd lock me away for insanity.

I left to talk to the innkeeper, but she couldn't be found. There weren't many I could ask, and I began to wonder if I had been the only one sleeping here last night. At long last, I found someone at the reception lobby who said they were the manager, but I didn't recognize her. This woman didn't look like she who I had seen being eaten in my dream, she didn't look anything like the woman who I'd met before. I asked this new woman where the other manager was, I even described her, but the woman standing before me said no one like that ever existed here. More frustrated than before, I asked for a new room and explained the storm damage in my current one.

This extra strangeness was what got me thinking that I should talk to someone about what I'd just been through. After being given a new room, I left and went out to talk to find and talk with my friend Brother Conleth at an old monastery that was within walking distance from the tavern.

I told Br. Conleth about Rutger and my dream, and he said I should give up these superstitions and ideas of make-believe. He said I was only plagued by too much imagination and too much alcohol and not enough time in service to God.

"Guerino," he said, "I will tell it to you in a way you might understand. What I say may not be what should be said, but what needs to be. I'll tell you what I may not dare say to others, but you'll know I'm being sincere. Guerino, what you experienced last night was nothing; it wasn't the truth, and you mustn't speak of those things to others, or they will take you for a fool or mad man. There are no magic forces, no powers of witchcraft, and no monsters of Hell. The Son of God hath already saved us and given us this world to live in peace and in servitude to the Almighty, who hath cleared away all the evils. Only our sins can keep us from God. Living is our punishment and our test, and yet a blessing most of all. Fear not monsters or dreams; fear God who is both unknowable and yet ever present with us. Think no more on illusions that spring from a weak and mortal brain. On this planet, there exists only the people and the animals which scholars and trusted officeholders have methodically studied and calculated and codified; nothing else survives, no ancient races, no old curses. What is here among us is only what God already made to perfection, and every one of those things has been recorded in books you yourself can examine. God is the only mystery. Rest. Spend time with Christ in solitude, away from the chaos of secular society. A worldly lifestyle and its material temptations can only make you addicted and preoccupied in mirage and fetishes and deceptions that are not real, things which are only physical matter, that turn the eye away from our loving Father. Science, reason, logic, and prayer will prove to you that there is nothing to fear and all you've endured is falsehood. Rejoice, for this is a sign that things will only get better for you. Every scrap of a human being is sinful: hair, flesh, muscle, curves, and eyes; yet, a human person should not be punished for the shape and guile of their bodies, but they should learn how best to temper them and return themselves to the original state which doth please the Holy Ghost. Take my advice. Find a place you'd feel safe. Go there. Spend your days there in service and contemplation for the Lord."

On my way back to the tavern, I had a lot to think about, and I was barely paying any attention to where I was going. I found myself in an old village filled with the throng and sounds of a gypsy festival.

A vixen ginger, with large brown eyes and long, curling hair, yanked me by the arm and pushed me behind an old hut. She was curvy and tall, taller than me, actually. Like pale honey, the warm, soft skin of her face and hands glistened. The golden light around her head dazzled her hair to look like fire. Light beige with rosy undertone, her ivory complexion reminded me of hazel or brass.

This woman said I looked lost and troubled and in need of a special fortuning. I asked for her name; in response, I got from this fox only a purr:

"Efrat."

Voluminous vermillion her veil, which fell from the crest of her head and hugged the round of her slight shoulders, was like a cloud of Mars. She whispered, said she was a gypsy fortuneteller, here until only midnight, and she said other things but in a language I couldn't understand. This gypsy gal in raiment scarlet with lengthy sleeves billowing, warned me that I was in trouble and in need of her advice. All I had to do was bring her to my place and pay her fee in advance. She was sniffing my throat, my face, and my chest; I had no idea what she was on or why she was acting like this, but I enjoyed it, to my surprise and embarrassment. In all this, there had been something about her glances and look that now made me think I'd be in more danger if I refused.

My heart yearned for closeness, and a secret need pulled at it as well: the lure of the esoteric, the forbidden. This would be my chance to see the other side of reality, to know if the rumors and legends of mysticism and magic were real in any way, and I was desperate to be proven right, to prove that there was more to this world than mundane physical ephemera and the promises coming from religious dogma. I became aware of a secret burden and hidden desire in me, more than ever before: to see if I could come close to anything resembling the supernatural or the underworld, to absolutely grasp a power to change my fate and master destiny and defy death. I had to take this chance to prove to myself that the supernatural was fake, or to see if there was something more than the mediocrity of mortal toil.

"How will you accomplish this? What neromealltach magic is this?" I asked.

Efrat said, "What? This is not black magic. No. What I have is real: the forgotten tools of unknown societies added to a darker science plus the more primitive mathematics that tap into the undiscovered water and sounds and hidden lines that have always been in the air around us, growing like branches of a tree indifferent to us; for they are the shapes and mists that have always been in subliminal link to thoughts, dreams, memories, genetic echoes, and telepathic buildup in amygdalae. There's so many waves and radiation zipping around us every second of the day, so much data, lights, lasers—and they're all invisible or undetectable by human senses—and these things have made it harder to feel effects of the other worlds and other beings, but sometimes all this activity, these invisible webs, might produce just the right passage for those that live within the radiation. Death is final, and there is no world after this, no form of life after you're dead. No heaven; you must understand. What some call "ghost," is just another natural and living organism made of dimensions, protoplasm, metafeoil, and appearances completely outside of human ken or animal. You see, there is no soul, only matter and will and energy and time, and these things can be crossed together with flesh and artifice to create true phenomena of power."

I had no idea what she was talking about, and I barely remember everything else she had said. Trust in her philosophy, I had little, but still I gave her the money she needed, and we went back to the tavern. I was ashamed in my curiosity and thoughtless actions, but I was so hungry for knowledge, hungry to make some try at connecting with the true machinery of the cosmos, that which people do not see is behind the curtains of our understanding and the limits of our minds. This would be my try at maybe changing things to help me, for I knew in my bosom that something mad and awful was approaching, and I didn' want to admit that there was an unknowable presence there with it, a feeling that forced upon my mind a sense of the mad and profane.

In my room, she covered the windows so all was blackness but the light of candles she produced from where I knew not. She started moving all the furniture around in a very curious configuration. Then, she sat me down in the center of the room, told me to be silent and still, and drew in chalk a large green pentacle around me. Around the outer perimeter of the pentacle, she drew a red square. Outside that, she made a triangle out of crystals showing an unusual luminosity. She finished this preparation by producing and fanning out a mysterious, metallic contraption; after which, she started drawing three white circles around her and then rubbing some similar like crystals on her forehead. All of this, the tools and this process, was completely unfamiliar and mind-boggling to me.

Efrat said, "The primeval artefact, our machine of travel and sight, has found us a connection to another other side of this mundane plane. Yes, I'm hearing the gates open for us. The ectoplasmic vapours and temporal hyperdimensional atoms have successfully joined my brain waves and cerebrospinal fluid; anon, my presence in this reality will be nothing but a conduit, and I will see everything that surrounds you. We will open a door and hope a guide enters, but it will not be anything that can be seen by human eyes or brains. We're too weak and have not the organs nor metafeoil for it. The hours aligned; the geometry balanced. The light—the sound—here is something now: Dubhdris Abbey, in Tarrytown. You'll go there. Must go. Nevertheless— wait, what is this place? Where have you brought me? What has happened? Old, they watch; old, they hear!"

I knew something wrong was here with us. Something horribly awry. When she started shrieking and convulsing, I screamed with terror and attempted to escape the room, but I was trapped in some invisible cage like a bug in a jar, with no hope of exit, and very little oxygen! Efrat's beautiful flesh was melting in ways no mortal flesh should be able, becoming a slime or wax; and oh how I bemoaned and sobbed out a lamentation stricken by rage and pity over the gross ruin and macabre decay of such beauty, her gorgeous body turning to ooze and pus, which left behind only her bloody skeleton with red veil billowing around red bones! I begged aloud for this to be a dream only, just a dream! I hoped a god could hear me out there, as I implored the night to take this episode away from my eyes!

A voice, more like an echo of thought, did come out of the skeleton gypsy, that voice a grim yawning blasting out from across oceans of despair decomposing betwixt forgotten infinity and incalculable annihilation. Voltaic caterwauling hemorrhaged across the all-around and within of the darkness surrounding. Electric notes of fear and angst flowed groaning amidst ethereal synth-like tones, as if projected and produced through illogical machinery of electronic nihilistic instruments of Tophet, which hurled the melancholy music over vast chasms of unknowable light-years and dropped into my very room!

"Thou hast been summoned," said it, "and thou hast been expected. Dubhdris Abbey awaits. The great ceremony must conclude with the chosen born of the servants of the most-high clerics!"

Horrid red lights appeared, I know not from where, and they did slip eerie around us. The dripping skull of Efrat seemed to look through me. A voice which should not have been did breathe out from the bones. Like a puppet or grotesque automaton, she dangled in the air, and somehow I knew with impulse and intuition that something else, something hidden, was controlling her and pushing her and carrying her with physical strength and solid mastery.

It said, "What unearthly device and foreign remnant were once, ere the long-distant primordial past, buried 'neath the land atop which now sits this here property—they keep open an interstice twixt the abysses and we. Now are the forgotten hours as one; minutes, arcminutes, and structures of space and time have been twisted where needed and put in alignment where necessary; they are in position to bridge parallel past and future akin to engineer an open path. Complete is thy maturity; O how has it ripened the hour! Invisible windows to other worlds follow thee, since thy blood is verily impatient for the ceremonial transformation, a moment for which thou wast chosen at birth!"

My continuous screams were to no avail. Every passing second made breathing harder and harder, until it was almost impossible. I gasped and tried to gain enough strength and air for a few final shouts for help.

"This can't be real!" I kept shouting. "Wake me up! Now! Wake up! Please, God, please! Help me!" I hoped there was a Christ to listen, but aware I was of my disbelief and lack of faith.

Electricity-filaments spun around me as smoke filled my invisible prison with a roar-of thunder and terrifying eruptions. My suffocation became unbearable and intense.

I must've fainted, and, when I awoke, I found myself in an unfamiliar, moonlit, cemetery. I had no chance to think or ponder, for I was immediately sprung upon by barbaric black dogs massive, things which chased me between the tombs and gravestones and monuments, things which slowly became more and more unwholesome as I ran and dodged. I don't even know how many there were when all around was too dark! Round and round, with all my strength and stamina I fought for my life. The baying and barking of the wild animals tormented every inch of my being. Against them my first defenses were stones I'd pick up and throw or the fallen branches I'd use as spears, but they had little effect. Next I found two old bricks and used that to keep them away when any got too near. Then a shovel, spotted against an old mausoleum, became my new weapon of defense. All the gates, thick and black spikes of austere guardianship, were too tall and heavily locked and chained to be used as an escape. I didn't even try to waste energy climbing.

There must have been someone here who could hear me screaming for help, because as I ran I thought I saw a face, though somewhat dumb and misshapen, stare down at me from an evil-lit miserable window poking out of the wall of a tower. A white and dismal claw-like hand pushed close the curtain. I must have been running for ten for fifteen minutes, trying to find a way out, to find escape from these dogs. That wretch at the window had seen me, I knew; but, did they call the cops? Did they do something? As far as I knew, they'd heard me and did nothing to help—and that made my suffering all the more mad and hurtful.

With huge paws did the dogs pound the mud, moss, grass, and cobblestone neath as they pursued me throughout the graveyard. I made for the Gothic structure that peeked between the rolls of fog and shadow. New moonbeams revealed a sign read: "Dubhdris Abbey."

Of course, there was no way I was ever going to win against the pack of savages. Overpowering me, they bit hard into my body, spraying blood, and dragged me through the now-opening doors of the abbey. Dark monks seized me and threw me into a dank coffin, locking it tight. I don't know what they did to me or even how long I was confined, practically buried alive like this. Extensive lengths of time stretched on for me in darkness. Repulsive music wailed and scratched, seemingly forever. My mutating body felt as if it were in acid as an abominable change lashed every screaming muscle and agonizing bone in my poor body.

I don't know how I survived, but I am certain I lost sanity, for everything that was happening and did happen after that has been one long horror from which I wished I could wake. There is no way for me to know with accuracy which part of this narrative is false and which truth. A never-ending claustrophobic darkness, the confused upside-down where I shed rivulets out panic-red eyes, consolation offered it to me none; for although I could see naught, oh how I was terrorized by some barbaric music climbing depraved, vain highs by mad frenzy overwrought for insanity resounding mounting dread!

Suddenly, I know not when after, the coffin lid was removed. The monks dumped me inside a sarcophagus filled with swampy slime. Terrible, morbid sounds and screeching and moans flooded ear and brain with bacchanalia preposterous.

From my prison am I now only to be released on full moons when the evil monks—Hipolit, Omar, and Bartel—command me to usher death and devastation upon a victim new and unsuspecting of their choosing. 'Tis their power I am under; total servitude: eat they let me almost whoever I wish, for a new despicable hunger hath replaced mine appetite; all I must is return afore dawn and bring enough blood back for the famigliarch of my inhuman bloodline, Abbot Alfred of Dubhdris Abbey. These bloody quests involve always me using my massive chiropteran wings in a flight with a hoard of beasts and animals; there are times when we must leave offerings to lifeforms which have sometimes been called "Grumocruths," which are too horrible to describe. Rutger is always among us, becoming more and more alien and unsettling to behold with every new flight through cracks between worlds and spaces unseen. Whenever complete are my nocturnal missions, forced back am I into the sarcophagus, where imbecilic drowses and grotesque dreaming impale me. I want to die though know not how! My body carries naught of the mortal world, instead of form and fortitude belonging to impossible dimensions parallel to that of humans; it obeys different laws and sometimes slips in and out of other realities unheard and forgotten, but always escape eludes me, and I'm never allowed far from this sarcophagus nor the abbey without the famigliarch's commands. I know that there are many others here like me, and there things hidden beside our tombs of which we do not know, nightmarish horrors unknowable and too terrible to be described; and if they should ever be disturbed, I know not what next would come of it or what they would do to the one who made offence.

Secretly, I've been writing this manuscript, about which none are aware. Even now are there times when still I try denial of what has happened to me. Even now, through all this, a broken part of me at dreary moments wants to believe my life has all just been a dream. Even as I'm writing this, I still can't believe what has happened. I reread everything I've written and I wonder if it was actually ever me who wrote. There are times in the dark when I'm completely lost to memory; my past eludes; and then, the traitorous shock, the memories must return in a rush of pain, and I am subjected to a flood of torments unbearable and unreasonable, where I must wait until the memories and agony fade back into numb madness; of course, I always wait, the horrid wait, the wait of anxiety and obsession, knowing that the memories will return, never knowing which are memories of dreams or memories of truth or of things to which I belong not. Should someone ever read this, then, please, find me, free me; learn me the truth.

I will lose all of my sanity and human senses. That time will come; feel it I do. I can only hope oblivion hits anon and quick with total death, or I will become like the others of my kind, nothing but a rotten member of a perverse scourge upon the world. For all this, if it all be true, I am sorry. Please, forgive me.

The End.

Fetch of Prismatic Froth

Before my will dissolves, I must explain how a bolt of woeful misfortune forever changed my ill-fated life and led me into greater distress. However, I realize now that destiny is a cursed illusion in a void manipulated by soulless chaos and unfathomable powers. All life on this planet is doomed to be the victim of random effects and outcomes caused by unpredictable horrors.

When I was eighteen years old, I began working in a local mill, but that didn't last long. I was fired because my manager wrongly assumed I'd been the one stealing tools. Months passed, I couldn't find another job, and I was still living with my parents.

An unforeseen, windy storm arrived and became astonishingly disastrous for many in the nearby area. Lightning hit my parents' house, while we were all still inside, and roaring fire consumed our home. We ran to escape the flames, but, by mischance, I got ensnared by fallen debris. I begged my parents to help me, but they ran out. I had to jump out a window to escape.

Frightened and upset, I ran until my legs wouldn't take me any farther. I didn't even know where I was going. I arrived on a silent, empty beach and noticed a towering mass of prismatic foam and bubbles that was sitting there alone. Never before had I found anything like this massive pile of white fizz and froth. I touched it, and immediately felt sick. The pile of foam started to melt and transform into an exact duplicate of me. I felt as if I had a painful fever and infection of the ears and throat. My twin dragged me into a dark cave, and then I blacked out.

When I awoke, I was in a hospital. No one believed me about the twin or the foam, and I never knew to where my double walked. My memories of what happened at the moonlit beach were hazy and almost incompatible, so I assumed it must have been a dream.

Ten years later, when my father died, he left me a mysterious house. I had never known about this place, and I was beginning to wonder what other things I didn't know about him. My father had always been a secretive man who was barely around. I didn't have any other living relatives or friends, so I went to live on my father's secret land.

Actually, my mother was alive, but she had been in a mental institution for several years and didn't want to see me. She had been suffering a bizarre illness and hadn't been the same person she once was. Though painful to accept, I tried to understand that she didn't want me in whatever remained of her life.

Another year passed. On one horrid night, before New Year's Eve, my double was standing above me as I was in my bed. I screamed, rubbed my heavy eyes, and then the intruder was gone. I told myself this bizarre phenomenon was nothing and tried to sleep, but terror choked me every time I shut my eyes. My whole body was shaking, my heart was slamming against my chest, and I prayed to God for salvation because I really thought I would die. I finally dozed off, but only for a brief time.

I awoke, walking through the dark woods surrounding my house. I didn't know how I got there. At the time, I believed I must've been sleepwalking because I didn't have control over my actions. I was watching myself acting like someone else, trying to slip back into myself but couldn't. My thoughts were unfamiliar, raw impulses determined by something far away.

I entered a forlorn graveyard and followed a pathway down into a dark, subterranean tunnel. I walked through a broken gate and discovered a chamber lit by dozens of melting candles. A black-cloaked figure, almost resembling a tall and lanky woman, was standing there, and I couldn't see her face.

She grabbed my arm and said, "Thither must we betake ourselves, to the repair of eldritch beings. Stand awed before the primeval gateway, whence mortals may chance beholding everlasting forces. With our offering of devotion have we thus remade our image to resemble spirits transcendental." Then, in a frightening manner, she was laughing.

I looked and was horrified to realize that the hand grabbing me was only bones. The woman was a humanoid skeleton, white-glowing and ethereal. I screamed when I saw her skull, and then pushed her away. Her cackling resounded throughout the damp tunnel as I ran for home.

Once inside, I still didn't feel safe. I dreaded the woman and the eldest beings of which she spoke, dreaded that they were already hiding inside the house. My growing fear worsened as I convulsed on the floor. I tried forcing my thoughts on real things I could control. Sleep finally took me away from my fears.

It was dawn when I woke, and still I lay on the cold floor. I wanted to return to my work, to forget the grim woman from my dream, for my sanity. Evening came, and I arrived at the house of a moneyed gentleman who had hired me to do a portrait of him.

When he opened the door for me, he looked shocked. He said, "What are you doing outside? Didn't I already let you in?"

I said, "No. I've only just arrived now. Who's in there with you?"

"I don't know. I thought it was you," he said. "What game is this? Stay inside."

Both of us were confused. He was telling me that I had already entered the house a few minutes ago, but I knew I had not. I didn't want to anger the affluent man, so I agreed with him and apologized.

I was feeling sick when I started painting. After an hour, I thought I would puke. Prismatic foam oozed out my mouth when I walked into the lavatory. I screamed when I looked into the mirror and saw my reflection vanished. Filled with unease, I gaped at the mirror for several minutes. When my reflection returned, it clawed at the glass, and then decayed into a cadaverous, zombie-like fiend that cackled at my terror. I shut my eyes and hurried out the lavatory.

Gasping for breath, I ran back to the room in which I had left the man. There, I saw the unfinished portrait now befouled. Someone had covered my once sublime artwork with dripping, red markings that were vaguely arranged like eerie, unintelligible writing. The image of the affluent man was now a dim smudge covered by abstruse, hieroglyphic symbols of unknown origin. Moving between the letters and symbols were red depictions of lobsters, crabs, clams, and wasps.

Terrified, I drew back from the painting. I certainly didn't paint those symbols, and I couldn't understand who would do this or for what mad design. I grabbed the ruined portrait and told the gentleman I needed to return another day to finish.

As I dashed out the door, I feared that I was truly becoming insane—not just me, the whole town, too. Pain and disasters had already been strangling this whole region for a full year. Earthquakes were becoming more frequent here, destroying many lives and families. More and more people had been getting sicker while an abnormal, malignant illness was continuing to spread town to town. Becoming a more often routine, groups of homeless people were fighting against punks in the streets. Mean vagrants and belligerent travelers had been passing through, attacking townsfolk.

I paid for information, trying to understand what people were doing and saying in the area. Many said that poverty and ill luck had come to the region because of some demon awoken by the earthquakes. Some were saying the bad luck was related to the arsonists and mass murderers who had never been caught. Passersby and locals with whom I spoke were grimacing and giving me rude looks as if I had done something awful. Maybe everyone was suspicious of one another.

I didn't know exactly what to believe. I couldn't guess as to what was causing the suffering. I told myself that luck rules our universe, puts its subjects in their places, chooses its happy champions, and deceives its fools and exiles. I believed that I could change my fate if I were brave and smart enough. I wanted to stop being lonely and scared.

When I arrived back inside my home, I again felt that I wasn't alone. I heard footsteps and whispers as if someone else was walking around the house. I had not been living with anyone. I was supposed to be the only one here. I had no guests and no family. I was always alone, so there should not have been anyone in the house with me. I checked everywhere and saw nothing.

Night came, and I was getting ready for bed when someone whispered from the hall. It was getting closer. I rushed to my door as something was running towards me and trying to get in. I screamed with terror as I pressed the door shut, but something slammed into it from the other side as I locked it. I was alone in the room, but someone had invaded my home. Someone was pounding on the bedroom door, which was driving me into wild fear. Screams sprang out from the other side of the wall and knifed my ears.

What slashed greater agony deep into my mind was the voice of that thing behind the door. It was speaking with my voice.

It said, "I remember the night mother wanted to kill you. She didn't know who you were and kept screeching you weren't her real son. Mother's still clawing at the walls in a mental institution. You'll not shut me out, too. Father left this cultic house to me, not you. Get out, fetch. Get out."

Mortified and terror-stricken, I was screaming for the invader to go away, screaming for him to leave me in peace and never return. His pounding on my door was an attack on my troubled brain and weak heart. The walls and floor of the room shook, as did my soul.

The man said, "They won't say it to your face, but everyone already blames father's cursed house for their bad luck and the illness spreadin' person to person 'round 'ere. They know what he prayed to inside these walls, what he found under this land."

Shivering in fear, I said, "You're lying. Go away. Leave. You use my voice, but you're not real. You speak confusion and falsehoods. This is a dream, a dream only."

The door finally opened. My double stood there in the doorway, and I fainted from fear and fatigue. My copy had an awful power over my mind. The sight of him was enough to make me black out from painful madness.

I awoke in a chamber I had never before seen. It seemed as if it was a secret laboratory and private library. Aflame candles were illuminating the room, so I assumed someone had recently been here.

While searching for a way out, I discovered an old, weathered journal filled with notes and things that had been handwritten by my father before he died. The things I read from it astounded and alarmed me. My heart burned with terrible uneasiness from it all.

Father had written about his investigations and blasphemous experiments with ghosts and the dead. His journal described how he joined an arcane cult before I was born. That cult had been studying and controlling many different types of hidden ghosts. He learned that there were ghosts who could give short life to inanimate matter, possess human beings, or merge memories together with those of their living victims.

In his notes, my father confessed to murdering many. He said his goal was infinite knowledge and to understand the ones who were far more important than humankind. It was through the ghosts of his victims that he learned about the existence of much older spirits who would sometimes visit our planet. He had become obsessed with finding one and studying it.

It took years, but he had finally discovered one of these ancient beings on a beach. It was not a spirit but was something completely otherworldly and paradoxical. He had followed it into a dark forest where it preferred to sleep beneath the ground. My father then built a secretive house on top of its domain and offered the beast sacrifices. This gigantic creature, which he adored, never appeared aware of his human existence, nor did it ever accept his gifts.

My father described, in the documents of his journal, that the gargantuan alien resembled a giant clam or a geoduck. However, when the monstrous shell opened, he had seen that inside was a kaleidoscopic, shapeless entity of ectoplasmic membranes too bewildering to belong to this universe. Projecting out from the interior of the shell were numerous, molten limbs. On rare occasions, the creature's breath and saliva could generate a frothy, toxic slime that would produce temporary imitations of anything it touched.

I recognized the foam about which my father had written. It reminded me of the stuff that had poisoned me on the beach. I remembered it becoming a copy of me after I touched it. Now, my memories of that horrid moment felt amiss and defiled, as if they had happened to someone else.

I couldn't read more. The rest of the journal was too cryptic and incomprehensible. Panicking, I ran away and screamed for help. I pounded on the old walls until I discovered a hidden door behind a curtain.

I ran out and followed a passageway into a large room illuminated by sconces. I stood at the edge of a yawning pit. A host of bats covered the rib vault ceiling. On the walls, inhuman hieroglyphics were glowing with brilliant white light. Robed figures walked down the stairway and circled around the brink of the deep pit. My double was among them.

I asked, "What is this place?"

My double turned to face me and said, "We're under our father's house. This is where his cult once gathered before they were crushed by the emanation of a grand visitor from another world. The deity carried clam-like lifeforms on its body, the same parasitic lifeforms our sickly father observed. We have awaited the return of the astral visitor and its migrating creations. You can still feel their dark aura and majestic shadows that've remained here and brought calamity and misfortune to the region and everyone in it."

I felt as if my brain was pounding against my skull. "Who are you?"

My double turned away and said, "I've tried to understand that. I've tried to make you understand, too. We need each other to live. Our memories are shadows and copies overlapping and melting together in each other's brains. We've been united for too long. What we are is an unfortunate accident, an accident that happened to a man who died and left behind two ghosts. Yes, one man died, but his spirit split into two. One of the ghosts is a parasite, the other a reflection. We've been continuing a dead man's life. Only now do I understand that our time ends tonight. If that is our fate, I want you to die first."

Deranged, my soul in agony, I screamed and lunged with boiling fury at my twin. The robed cultists grappled me and pinned me to the floor. I cried and yelled for mercy, in vain. I was helpless and outnumbered.

Everything around us began to shake. This underground chamber was trembling. The swarm of bats screeched and flew out. Pillars and arches fell and crushed some of the cultists. I used this opportunity to escape and ran up the stairway. My twin and the remaining cultists were right behind me, still chasing. I only escaped them because the floor broke apart, and they fell down to the bottom of the deep chasm below. I had grabbed a ledge and pulled myself up.

When I finally escaped the house, I saw it fall down into an enormous fissure that suddenly and violently split the ground. Eerie clouds obscured the moon, and nighttime shadows hurried over everything. Fire jumped out of widening cracks in the ground. I evaded the falling, burning trees as I ran through the fiery woods.

A horrid form swung down from behind me and flailed around. It swiftly struck the ground beside me and produced such powerful gusts that I fell. I wasn't certain what it was, but it vaguely looked like a huge, strobing proboscis. Then, another form came down from above and whipped the ground around me. The second limb resembled a flashing trail of pearly eyes connected by phantasmagoric vapor. These massive appendages ripped apart the ground and shattered trees effortlessly.

Praying that I wouldn't get crushed, I covered my face with my arms and closed my eyes. I hated how unprepared I was, hated how all I could do was beg and pray. I hated this unavoidable force that was so much stronger and more massive than me. This experience shocked me with such feelings of sheer terror and insignificance that I couldn't move. I could've died of fear. I was reminded of how defenseless and small humans were in this universe filled with forces of unpredictable misfortune. I knew that human beings were an unprepared species and couldn't survive for much longer against the simple actions made by inhuman powers that acted without concern for things so minuscule as humanity.

I never saw to what abomination those limbs belonged. I don't even know if those were the appendages or the weapons of a living creature. They could have been parts of something else entirely. I wondered if those things belonged to different creatures or if they were connected to one colossal body much larger than any animal on this planet.

When I opened my eyes, those terrifying limbs had disappeared. I arose and heard bloodcurdling sounds almost indescribable. I looked up and saw an effervescent plume rising above the burning trees.

Raving and deranged, I must've run for hours. By mishap, I stumbled into a moonlit cave. I don't understand much about what happened next. I entered a hidden cavern within and heard someone commanding me to dig. I obeyed, by instinct, and dug through the muddy ground with my hands. I couldn't see very clearly, but I knew I found something remarkable.

I pulled something out that had been hidden beneath a mucky mound of seaweed and mossy stones. I dragged it outside into the moonlight and gasped when I understood what I had unearthed—a gruesome, human corpse.

Holding the dead man's hands, memories returned to me, and I remembered who he had been. I cried over the corpse of this man, a man I had killed and had been mimicking since the time I dragged his poisoned body into the cave. This corpse had been a man who died and left behind two ghosts of himself. His spirit had shattered. One of his ghosts had been altered by the presence of his fetch—by me—who somehow never let go until tonight.

Heartbroken, I was disgusted with my loathsome nature and pointless life. I was a debased and inhuman creature having no family, no purpose, and nothing important to offer. As my awareness was slipping away, I felt more like a broken machine, a fleeting copy of a human being. I feared my evil desires and horrid choices.

I once thought that chance, luck, and one's fortune determined everything. Now, I see how even those are illusions and perversions of reality. Chaos and misfortune mock and mimic all things. Those soulless designs of destiny are only reflections of ourselves as we go back to darkness. To live is to endure catastrophes and accidents, to become the pain that wounds us. Our world is made of unwitting coincidences, without resolution. All of this is inconsequential to the unknown beings whose presence makes us insane and cursed. The everlasting and otherworldly entities, those who twist reality, do not care about our fate.

I brought the man's corpse to the police and asked for some things to write my story, so that I could tell everyone what I knew. My legs turned to foam. My skin became small bubbles. Horror was my final emotion as I watched myself melt. Strange worms and wasp-like things came up from the scum. Someone will find me, and I'll be a corpse of prismatic froth and filth.

The End.

Grumocruth

Dear Dr. Alan Mikolajczak,

I am sending you the items you asked for. I have preserved the originals to the best of my abilities. I will also be sending other copies and photos of these findings to the museum after I speak with police. Do with these whatever you deem best. Show them to the proper legal authorities, if you wish. I have tried, but with no success, to contact those who might know what these are. By next Monday, you should receive the "Grumocruth" statuette and a strange photo I discovered among these materials.

The following materials are only copies or transcriptions of texts I found at a makeshift shrine adjacent to a swamp in New York. I've copied them and labeled them as "*Item I*," "*Item II*," and "*Item III*." My opinion is "Item I" and "II" appear related. "III" is my best attempt at transcribing what had been written on a severed hand still holding the materials when I had found them. I will now present all three items below; see the subsequent pages.

Yours truly,
Dr. Ludwig Hayes

Item I

Always the same was it everywhere. Wirra, wirra, how painful, a spear through heart and guts was this pain of seeing more and more cynical strangers pushing and penetrating into vulgar, sordid streets, more and more by the night, so many of them like an epidemic, and, yet, none of them offered kindness nor prayer to me! Hoary, knotted hands reached from the ignoble shadows of the garbage-stuffed alleyways to snatch any coins that would slip through my fingers. Glaring directly at me, into me, through smoke and fumes were oily, dark eyes barbarically wide and hate-swelling, orbs vexed and dribbling with murderous-hunger, following me. Riots and rampage vandalized land and sky with flames and smoke, leaving a span of cataclysm glistening of the filth and the ash of doom and a melancholy ravishing and replacing beautiful monuments or innocent homes. Didn't matter where I went, the city always seemed to follow me, like I was walking down the passages of one big, long labyrinth of urban ghetto stretching and expanding across the globe.

I had to make a change. When August came, I went to central Italy. I found lodging with an old woman and her middle-aged sons who offered to pay me for my help with their gardens and livestock, which could only be accessed far away from the house by climbing a steep, narrow footpath up hills and through harsh woods.

Theirs was a horrible, poor home of simple and unadorned walls; rustic, plain rooms; and an infuriating combination of lifeless, modernistic design bleached with postmodernist "architecture" matching the dozens of nearby homes squeezed together in the lowest parts of town.

In their smallest upstairs room, they had an open wood chest filled with items of the most bizarre, unsettling qualities: rotten papers, moldy books, slimy urns, gross-filled jars, soiled blankets, outlandish effigies, and an even weirder statuette resembling nothing I'd ever before seen. All sides of the statuette were written in a rare kind of medieval Italian, a kind reminiscent of old Sicilian and Tuscan, mixed with Latin and something other, an odd language I couldn't understand. I had never told the old woman or her sons I was ever in this room, but, ever since that one time, they always kept the door to that room locked, and never again did I enter or was allowed entry. In truth, none of them ever spoke of it or answered any question that might reveal any information about that mystery and what was inside. Of what was written on the sculpture, all I remember translating with any scrap of clarity was one real peculiar word: Grumocruth.

One day, while walking alone through these woods, it was Ferragosto, so everyone else in the small town was away for the holiday feast, I heard the eeriest sort of moaning or crying. Excited by the mystery, I ran toward it and searched for the source of that most wretched keening. As I followed the sound, I heard something as if someone was running and pushing through leaves and branches.

Not many minutes passed—I remember because I had to check my watch after feeling like ten hours had gone by—before I found myself in a part of the woods where the hills, now much more steep and knotty than the ones previous, became undulate and heaving maniacally. The footpaths had disappeared, and the trees were dense and thick. I felt like someone had kicked all the life and strength out of me. I was barely able to move my arms or legs. The branches here curled and twisted around the thick trunks with alien proportions. There were what looked maybe like pine trees but much more unsettling for their lurid quality and an attitude they had as if telling me they knew I was there. Uncanny, strong winds rushed in. The crying became a shrill and steady mewling or soughing swishing in the distance. The clouds began to warn of a coming storm. Arms of the spruce and oaks battered against me as I ran this way or that. The fanged rocks of land bit my heels as the mossy lips of the leafy ground skinned its teeth beneath me, and the woodland floor snarled, leered, grinned, and sneered under my aching feet. Chestnut trees quavered in the lash of weird air. I lost all sense of direction under that verdant vault beneath which was a mangle of maple trees and fallen beech.

Through a gorge I forced myself into a pathetic run and soon discovered the entrance to a tall cave, from which there erupted screams. Once inside, my stinging mind warned me that something was there with me, but I still saw nothing but an empty cave. Then, the screaming and crying stopped. Even with a light, there was nothing there. I needed rest that instant. Besides, the cave provided a fine enough shelter, since demanding rain had now started to fall in heavy strokes. A ray of thrill and sublime curiosity illuminated my senses. I wanted to know more and see more. How could I abandon such an adventure? No one had told me there were caves around here. It was exciting stuff. The rainfall was striking thicker by the second.

Something like wind pushed me to the ground and the rain just outside the mouth of the cave, for just a moment, began to act strange, as if the showers were striking a physical object out there; again, I saw nothing and there was no one else with me. I began to suppose the storm was becoming more agitated, so I just waited for it to be over and stayed in the cave. I also thought I had slipped perhaps. Behind me was just a pile of bricks, stones, dirt, marble, and tall slabs of rock; it was as if something have caved in or fallen to destruction. There was nothing exciting or interesting about the cave. That's when I fell asleep, waiting for the storm to die.

Once awake, and the storm was over, I exited the cave and searched for a way back to the town. Refreshed, I walked out and looked for the home of the old woman and her sons. Quickly, I found a tall monument telling me that I had reached into Molise. That seemed strange to me, because I didn't remember the old woman's place being anywhere near Molise, but I knew I must just be tired and not thinking clearly. It was such a strange state of mind that came over me, like I was losing my grip on direction, the hours, or my location. After eating, I asked some townsfolk about the cave, and the answers I got were startling and upsetting.

Most said the cave was a myth or folktale, they were angry at me for talking about it and wouldn't go beyond that. I really had to push and beg for answers. Finally, some said that the cave was the place where kidnappers and gangsters would hide or bury bodies. Two or three of the oldest men warned me that the cave was home to goblins, imps, and fiends. From what they said: even before it was used by those monsters, it has always been a home of great evil and crimes of the most perverted and blasphemous, a place where crones and their daughters would carry out the blackest hecatombs and carnage of cannibalism, infanticide, saturnalia wassailing, and breeding and copulation with early prehuman ones and the antediluvian creatures of forgotten stars and planets. Rumors suggested that sometimes, even in modern days, the old ones come and snatch men and women and force them to participate in orgies. Some of the more fantastical stories were those suggesting how the elder animals haunting the place were primitive creatures with tools and mental abilities that could let them go to other realities or exchange will and memory, like weirder kinds of astral projection and possession. After I asked if they had ever told these stories to others, they said it was no good, said no one would believe. I heard someone say that a few people had gone there and found nothing. In fact, they said the only reason why they were telling me was that it appeared I had already been tainted by the place, and they wanted me to leave before I harmed others or myself.

It was only after hearing these horrible and ridiculous tall tales that I remembered something about my time in the cave. I couldn't believe that I had actually forgotten such a thing. And now, feeling the dark memories burn across my mind, it was as if I was reliving the whole incident again but for the first time. My eyes wandered back to the woods and brought me there again, back at the cave, in gloomy reverie or warped somnambulism. Before the cave entrance was a monument, or sculpture of some kind, strangled and smothered by bramble, thorns, sharp vines, thistles, and ivy.

From what I could see, the monument, now badly damaged, was of a giallo antico or some other kind of yellow marmorean. Of what was left, it seemed to depict a seductive woman's willowy yet ripe torso of plentiful bosom and sylphlike wasp waist. Her legs demonstrated a scheming and arduous bearing. All other pieces of the body had been broken, decayed, or fallen off at some point in the faraway past. Other parts of the statue were much too thickly covered with vines or just so bizarre and faded that I can't honestly say what they were supposed to be at one point. For a moment, I almost thought it reminded me of something I might see on a gargoyle or Roman grotesque of a Sphinx, Lamia, or Harpy; although, I can't really say as to why, only that the proportions and the pose all whispered of a Saturnian bloodthirstiness. A kind of inscription at the plinth base was still visible, the weeds and vines had avoided this part of the piece, and it looked like no language I had ever seen before; actually, it reminded me of the writing I saw on the Grumocruth statuette.

I reached into my pocket, got my phone, and found the photo of the monument inscription. How could the memory be true? How could I have forgotten something like that? And how did I forget that I'd taken a photo of the inscription?

There was nothing else I could do here. I tried to get more answers, but everyone was done talking. I couldn't get a word out of anyone about the cave, the monument, the statue, or anything else about the local folklore. There wasn't anything about it online or in any database either.

When I returned to them, something about the old woman and her sons had been disturbing me. But it was more than that, it was their home too, which had me spooked. I would always wake up yellowish, fatigued, and dizzy, which I tried to fix with more and more espresso each morning; so, perhaps that was why I felt so distressed and paranoid about everything. As for my three hosts, they seemed more youthful, more alive and sanguine. I think something was wrong with my eyes too. A few times, while I was looking at the old woman, light didn't play right around her, as if she were somehow standing in the way of a large fire. After a few nights, I was so delirious, I thought she resembled a beautiful mistress. It excited such emotion in me that I would even have dreams of her. My irrational mind was so agitated that my dreams became more terrible, and each time I would image the three becoming as vermin crawling to my bed and sitting upon me.

I couldn't stay there any longer. Things were just becoming too awkward. I left as soon as I could and went to see a doctor. I was told I'd be fine if I had a few days of better sleep. Afterwards, I returned to my New England office.

I wanted to ask a friend about helping me understand my photo. There was a chance someone else might have discovered things that could give me the proper clarity.

As I recall, it was in the first days of December when I entered the city of Salem in that sage American state of Massachusetts. I was here to see my friend Norwood, a hard-working whiz of languages and the study of antiquities, who finally had time to chat with me. I had already told him my story and everything I'd discovered or heard about the statuette, cave, monument, and the folklore from those Italian townsfolk.

Norwood told me that he had been very busy most recently with studying ancient ruins on the borders of Iran, Pakistan, and Afghanistan that matched similar ruins he had discovered years before in Ireland, Italy, and Egypt. What he had found in those places was very similar to what I had found in Italy. Norwood explained he had encountered what looked like the remains of an ancient Indo-Aryan civilization far older than he had ever thought possible; it was a civilization ruled by a sort resembling the Nuristani, Indic, and Dardic peoples showing racial, cultural, and genetic strains of the Mongol, Ainu, Han, Evenki, and Manchu. At one of these ruins, he had met up with a Mr. Barnabas Zangari who seemed to be interested in this lost society's rituals of a type of necromancy connecting ancient Hinduism with a technological bend of animism. One day, Mr. Zangari was just gone, leaving behind everything including money and personal valuables. At their camp, he had left behind many journals, notes, and incomprehensible volumes. This sudden departure put a halt to the research project, giving Norwood time to visit me.

There was something about what Norwood was saying, or maybe it was just the way in which he was talking to me, that made me feel like he wasn't telling all the truth.

When Norwood had finished translating the inscription in my photo to English, this is what it came out to:

AH! Demogorgon on charnel heap and horde accepted the sacrifice of one thousand times one thousand, that burnt offering, and on Succoth wove it we with blood kalasha and true qabalah. AH! This transmundane dharma forever and forever. Vandal and ingest. AH! Drunk converted of endless wheel. From the first chaos returns the Grumocruth, avenger destroying giaour and kafir. All-hetaerae, ravish and violate. Arisen Grumocruth. All-hierophant. AH! Grumocruth lift abyss and topple sky. Grumocruth, our god. Remember this miracle. AH!

After I was finished reading the translation, Norwood produced an envelope, in which was a letter.

He said, "I took this here letter with none wise to me doin' so. It'd belonged to Mr. Zangari; but he's gone now, lost after he brought the elbosum and unearthly to this side. He used the words 'n' tools o' that forgotten religion for which we'd longed to understand. I saw that ealulych corpse which did jump out the tomb 'n' took 'im. To bloody hell with that machine o' his! I destroyed it rightly after 't tried a get me; I swore I'd never tell a soul. Zangari be on that other side now. Ye should read 't now, me sembosemmcyn, me lad, for 'twould seem ye been caught in this nasty web o' neromealltach 'n' nightmares too, now that you'll be wantin' sooth o' all 'is."

"You jest! How can any of that be true? It is silly superstition and worthless fiction! In truth, you couldn't possibly expect me to believe you. Am I to trust the folklore and fantasies of peasants and madmen? The monument I found and its inscription could not possibly mean what you say it does. It is all rubbish, and you know it. That inscription, the one I found, was written to impress people with dream legends, to fool slaves into servitude, to scare people—nothing more! Or else, it was simply a joke, one of which you seem to have taken too far. There are no gods, no ghosts, no inhuman monsters, and no cult murdering and molesting people en masse for their pagan lords! You have no proof!"

"Read 't, mon! Read the letter ol' Zangari left behind!"

I read the letter aloud, and, when I was finished, left in an outrage.

I didn't believe any of it. Don't think I did. I'm only writing about all this because it was the weirdest experience of my life, and perhaps one day I should like I look back on it with amusement.

Item II

Dear Mr. Barnabas Zangari:

I hope this letter finds you well. It is with respect that I've written to you, but it is of somber matters of grim significance that must be communicated. You may not remember or even understand, but we have once met. Ever since our first encounter, I've been admiring your work and research from afar, from behind and beneath the shadows where you couldn't see me. You're so close now, so close to the truth. I've been looking for someone like you. You're not afraid to plunge into death to pull back something of deepest significance, but none of your experiments have worked. Mr. Zangari, I know; I know all about your laboratory and the ruins you've been using as your secret vault of the macabre. I've been following you as you searched for a way to pull back the mundane veil, to see the hidden things beneath reality in a parallel world of which only a rare few can ever learn. I've followed you as you went looking for answers to the mysteries and secrets of mystagogy, occult galvanism, esoteric thaumaturgy, and the black arts. You want to talk to the dead, but you've failed to do so; you failed to find any evidence that a soul exists. Your searching has left you dry and empty. You're losing faith. You lack that dark conviction needed to go farther. You're discovering that things are not as you wanted them to be. There is no magic, only the cold and uncaring void and its unbreakable principles. But I also know, in your desperation and long investigating, that you've come across the remains of an ancient race long-thought to have been extinct. It has lead you onto a trail of murders and other grisly evidence pointing to an ever more-ancient cult of "Grumocruth." And so, now you're wondering if this "Grumocruth" cult can be your link to figuring out a way to explore other worlds and communicate with things better left ignored or dead.

Please, call me Ademaro. I can tell you—I've learned nothing about the soul or the dead. I've seen nothing that could tell me there exists a God. I've seen no evidence of ghosts or devils. What I have seen are the material things that have always lived here, physical things that have survived and never went away, only hidden away from mortal vision. I once wanted to believe these things were only hallucinations or nightmarish fancies of a deranged sod. I will no longer be able to deny the truth of this miserable business.

Why am I writing to you about all this? I won't be here much longer, Mr. Zangari. The things I have learned, of the world and of myself, have made me only wish for a release from all this pain and fear. Police are looking for me, and it won't be long before they finally catch me—they'll find only a corpse.

I had tried to live a normal life, but there are things that mankind was never meant to explore or understand, things that would change anyone after learning of them. This is the end of the journey of the human race, and the alien powers will take your skins and carry on without you. I'm not completely heartless. I can't live with what I've done or what I know I'll do. Those monsters get inside you; they use you. Can't you see it? Surely, you must understand. I am sure you will, in time. Humans think they are alone here on this planet with only the plants, bugs, and animals; they think that humans conquered and understood all there is to. Humans think their thoughts, but not alone. The outer beings are always listening. While you sleep, they crawl into you. O how they love human blood, human dreams, human screams. I see them now, and I'm seeing them more and more each night. But, I forget that I should consider myself as human in all this too, no? That old race of outer things, they made me a sire of otherworldly products, and they gave me the blood which made me like one of their slaves. Whatever they had put inside me, these things show me what has always been invisible around us.

How did I first discover all this? I guess I should say that it all began when I decided to leave home. It was no use—I just had to, simply had to, get out of that impoverished house, that penurious and squalid web unfit to ever even be called a "house" or a "home," the previous occupants of which had been slovenly lowlives who had let the rustic and shoddy formation go to rot and insulting vulgarity long-before I had ever occupied the decrepit property. No, I wouldn't even dare call it a "place," for it, my hometown abode, was more a "bulge" haunted by long-established pain, an ancient poverty in all respects.

I needed time to be alone and far away, for a very long time. At least, I didn't want to speak with anyone who had previously known me. My life had never been a happy one. I'd been wasting too much time as a no-account—"but all that would finally be the past!" so I told myself. Now was my time to go out, to try something different, be something different, to try an adventure of some kind. I wanted to become a man of respect and intellect. Maybe, I thought, I should like to make a true friend.

After too many years of saving up cash from degrading jobs ranging from the menial, the retail, and those of the harshest manual labor, I finally had enough to take the big trip I always wanted. I became a travelling photographer and took my camera with me everywhere. I was a man of thirty, and it was about time I get out there and see everything I ever wanted to. I would go out for a year and do whatever I wanted. I only knew English, but I wouldn't be staying anywhere long enough for me to need any other languages. I would bring with me books of translations, and I'd have online notes telling me how to get around anywhere and stay safe.

I started my trip by going to London, England in January and moved place to place on foot, by bus, by train, on boat, or through air. As a side project, I was freelancing and selling my photographs online. Whenever I assumed my funds were dangerously low, I'd earn coins or banknotes along the way by selling picturesque photographs to impatient tourists. I'd even been offering assistance to those who needed help moving and transporting heavy objects. I encountered many people this way, sharing many truck-rides and boat-rides with so many different people; however, all of them were much too surly and aloof, and they made negligible conversation with me, so I never had a chance to make any friends. These people just wanted to do the work, pay me, and be gone. No talk. No emotion. No warmth. None of those things from them. No matter how hard I tried or how many different ways I attempted to make conversation or be friendly, the people I was working with were distant and silent. So, that's how it was, and I was an outcast still.

Nevertheless, it was such a breathtaking experience, to see real beauty and sophistication immortalized through architecture and art, things so different from what I had known back home. I wanted to become a part of it, to preserve and protect all the beauty and elegance that made my heart soar up into a fantastic vault of bliss and passion. For the first time, I was in a land that seemed to know me and to feel as I. The beautiful buildings and natural terrain around me, in this world so new to me, awakened a power I had never felt before. For once, I didn't feel like I was just another insignificant lost in the trash and filth. I was surrounded by grand displays of poignant emotion and bracing craftsmanship promising the wondrous possibility of anything and nourishing eternity. The ancient roads and eldest statues were proof of humankind's goodness and joyful purpose.

For Holy Week, I was in Andalusia of Spain. During this time, I was also in and out of Murcia and Madrid. I did not stay as long as I had wanted, for it was here that I began to notice I was being followed by something ominous.

Hunchbacked, gaunt persons stalked me for whatever unknown reason; sometimes I would find dripping-red bags right outside my door, and off in the darkness yonder would be the forms of those twisted persons peeking from behind something to watch me. I would never open the bags, I didn't want to touch them nor bring them into my room, but I would always report to the police; though, the authorities did nothing, even after I'd shown them photos. Such negligence and impotence. They stated they never found any evidence of such things or any bags or any people like the ones I'd described, said they weren't allowed to do anything even if they wanted. We all were helpless and could afford no avail.

As lonely as I was, I didn't want to get close to the twisted ones who were following me, for they seemed unsavory and disturbed. I knew better then to get involved with such dangerous things. I wanted a traditional, upstanding life of refinement and repose. The lepers following me and delivering bloody sacks had a criminal appearance of betrayal and contamination. Who would want them but the most perverse and loathsome? Even when I had called out to them and tried to communicate, they said nothing, but they did leave me with an air of malice razing my heart. For days and nights I worried when would be the next time they'd come or if they would ever stop following me.

Thus, I left for Egypt and there explored in disillusion the festering streets glowering and squirming to my every step within the decadent, clamorous rookery of Cairo. Dust and sparks twirled around me as protests and violence took dominion. Loosened dogs and wild jackals prowled across yards and roads, as if knowing of some horrible and intense end where they could soon be free to play, kill, and howl was coming.

After taking me to see pyramids, museums, and markets, my hired guide brought me to an affordable but dingy hostel where I had planned to stay for only one day. But it was later that night, while I was in the communal kitchen, an old black-veiled woman grabbed my arm and begged me for money. I hadn't the faintest notion about whence she'd come, because, before, I'd thought I was the only one there. Fearing she was attempting to rob me, as I could feel her mushy, bony hands slipping and poking up and in and down all over my body, I pushed away from her and locked myself in my tiny room. Weird sounds came from the jiggling door, which I dared not open nor approach.

Not an hour later, myself lain on a divan chair out of fear of contracting something from the foul-stained cot, I heard a quizzical tittering scratch the darkness and a creepy whispering escape the pipe-cluttered, xanthic walls, these ill-natured and vitriolic enclosures, of the decayed shaft, this so-called "room". I couldn't stop my thinking, panicking, worrying someone was calling me, saying my name, knowing me, mocking me in meanness loudening and more louder.

"Ademaro! Ademaro! Ademaro!"

I jumped from the divan after a venom-gurgling cackle heinous raced forth from the outside behind the odious, orange-curtained window. Turning on the lights, I hurried around the room, looking for a way to use something here as a weapon. There dashed sounds warning of something forcing open the window! I tried the door, but it refused me! Trapped! Somehow, the door had become locked from out there and here, with no way of escape into or out of this horrible cell!

I grabbed my phone and called for the police with shaking, fright-worn fingers. I looked down at the numbers and tried not to drop it. What happened next must have only been a dream, for it was all too repulsive and unprecedented. In a great fear, I must have really been losing it.

When I turned up my head, a grotesque, bloody form climbed inside through the broken window. Glass shattered on the floor. I pulled at the door, but it wouldn't open; it would only hiss out a spray of goop or bitumen and malodorous resins. This death-reeking mucus slipped under the door and spread across the floor, even attaching like flesh or fungi to the door hinges and jambs. I turned and looked at the intruder behind me. What I saw was enough to make be believe I must have fainted from fear combined with the noxious gas pouring into the room.

The next morning, I found myself at the base of a disgusting pile of trash in an alleyway. I looked back in memory and thought the torture I'd experienced the night previous was a dream, but something about all of it, that night, the wild experience I had in my room as the intruder came in, something about what had been happening felt so real and pungent. Yet naïve as I was then, I still wasn't certain if all those things actually did happen. I thought I could have had only been hallucinating. But as to what had caused this reaction, I couldn't explain. I wanted to find a logical explanation, searching my memories, but found nothing comforting. I could only assume, given the likelihood of such an event, if someone had drugged me or used some dangerous chemicals on me, that that could have been the cause of what I had felt and witnessed. I didn't know who would do something like that to me. Then again, I began to wonder, might have the beggar woman done something to me, perhaps because I had rejected her, because I had refused to give her money? Or perhaps she was already using something on me that failed to affect me until I was already in my room; maybe, she had used something to make me forget she had tried to rob me, and whatever she used on me could have given me a nightmarish reaction? I was eager to believe my memories of the otherworldly bacchanalia were most probably the creation of a hazardous mixture of ill emotions, bad nerves, bad air, a mind of over-stressed psychology, and indigestion, brought on by contaminated food and impure water, that I hallucinated to such a nightmarish degree before my blackout.

I only started writing all this down because there was something inside me that knew this was important, something I couldn't shake. My mind rejected the memory, and yet it told me there was something real to it all, something that others should know about. O how my belly burned and raged against me as I wrote this out at first. Flames licked the insides of my stomach. I was on the precipice of madness and intoxicating frenzy because of that night, the haunting and maddening memory of that hideous night, that hideous thing! I felt like I'd be forever sick, like I'd never be well again. My body was hot and my hands were lethal. I knew I was going more insane, most mad; just remembering that awful dream, if it was a dream, was killing me! I had never been more afraid of the unknown yet simultaneously aggressively seeking the olden techniques of the greatest mysteries. I didn't recognize myself as I was; I was afraid I might do something awful, and maybe, I stewed, I had already committed atrocities I could not remember.

But why should I be alone in my shame, for are not all of us, we mortals, puppets and receptacles for the truer world around us and all its formless powers? Is being human not being aware of ourselves ugly and powerless? We see all the vast potential of the universe but are incapable of using or understanding any of it. Have we not become, simply put, aware that we are a joke, an accidental filth incapable of meaning but hoping, in vain, to one day become something more or other? Has not humanity become prideful and ironically narcissistic of their own ignorance and oblivion that it, and those of the human race, has thrown itself into a wild swell of stark fornication and crude dissipation? Knowledge or ignorance, all lies! No safety! No escaping change!

What I have to say now may offer some insight about what is to come. I've realized that the night of monsters was more than a dream. The truth I have learned is now my doom. I can't be alone with this; I've got to share it; I've got to hold it out for others to carry with me. It's just not right that such impossible-seeming and unavoidable forces of change can come to someone and ruin everything. I'll only state what I think happened, what I might remember.

Again, remember, I can only describe it in ways that make sense to me. I have no idea what was really going on, and my descriptions, my words, can never fully describe nor fully explain the things I had actually seen. I know it seems confusing, but nothing has been certain ever since that night; there may even be a chance my entire life has been a lie. I can only give you things I've learned as I now look back on everything in hindsight.

Now, back to that night in the hostel—as I wrote earlier, I saw the intruder behind me, and the sight called raving, stark fear to rip through all my being. My trembling legs were ready to collapse as the ambiguously humanoid invader rose up on its bare bristly feet of crooked toes, insectival talons, and hooked claws. It had a strange appendage grown out of its left side, a repulsive limb resembling a greatly overgrown membranous wing or perchance a gathering of gigantic spidery legs webbed together in gangrenous flesh; it's hard to remember or even give a definitive description of that repulsive part. In one hand it waved a scimitar; in the other, a wicked kirpan. Tall and long-legged was this towering thing, most likely female, somewhat resembling a corpulent old woman, with thick gray and black patches of hair grown here and there on her vitiligo-laced body of yellowish-sable skin. She wore no clothes nor covering beyond a high, simple comb under a ragged black mantilla flowing down from her head to her shoulders. Red crud leaked out of her ears and the corners of her eyes and mouth. Clusters of proboscis-like, sucking mouthparts with tetter-clad lips, these weedy and tensile tubes, attached at their bases to her loins and chest, reached out to grab me with the help of flapping tentacles. From her mouth dangled the mangled corpse of a human infant.

She was shrieking and screaming things I couldn't understand. I only remember that which she repeated in sometimes guttural and sometimes shrill tones: "Grumocruth! Grumocruth! Grumocruth!"

Her weapons dripped a queer, clear liquid steaming and reeking a cloying, surgical, narcotic, musty malodor. The second the slender-sharp tip of her pulsating dagger pierced my skin, I was totally lost to madness, hallucination, and schizophrenic dissociation. I heard the unwanted thoughts of a perverse, primal part of myself, one with whom I'd only been familiar in my more worser nightmares. There came so much screaming, some of it coming from me.

I remember being carried and dragged across the heights and steeps and rooftops of Cairo; then, there came the black of utter night. And next, there was the subterranean pit of Walpurgis Night evils and blackest revelry of beasts too shocking to mention, where the most fearsome, potent creatures commanded and had their way with me, and they fed me all the dross and innards of things I dare not mention here. The hags and brutes seemed to display their naked forms in reverence to a "Grumocruth," and they wrote this name in stone and wood on which they poured both human and animal blood alike. They forced me to write it too and to dance around the impossible-enormous obelisks.

I looked upward upon the startling-tall pillars, on which clung gigantic creatures, part-sphinx, part-trichopteran abominations also having a multitude of antennae, tendrils, tentacles, and proboscises. These giant horrors had what appeared to be an armament of the most awful and devious instruments and devices with which they created terrifying music or something like music resounding around us. Their tools made nightmarish, hypnotizing sounds, which I recognized to be somewhat like sounds not much different from those that could be produced by screaming or barking, but this noise also was like agonized electric sounds of scratching and squeaking, and adding to this tumult were cacophonies of craving and obscene voices. Chirring joined the sounds of chimes and tam-tams with salacious hedonism. Mocking warbling joined the castanets. A vitious stimulation of shamisen and bells soared beside the clamor of gongs and xylophones. A din of rattles and belching rushed to the side of a frenetic synthesizer of alien vibrations. What sounded like shakuhachi and weeping mounted upon a trance of sistrums and mbira. Kotos, zithern, and zurnas made their nymphal calls across this deep calamity, this "wergianiht." That is exactly what the carnal music was, a wergianiht, a fitting term for a disgusting nocturnal cacophony of orgiastic terror and debauchery, a word I learned from those old enough to remember hearing the moonlit clangor of more ancient, forgotten beings in their estrus-madness. I don't have the stomach to say what else I participated in or what more they did to me.

After I learned the truth of that night, after I could no longer deny the changes and vicissitudes upon my existence, I remember at first planning to throw myself off a cliff. Oblivion can be a comfort, if one could only realize that there is no hereafter, no Adonai. Abraham's bosom is nothing, is it not? For why else do such impossible misfortunes occur to someone like me? Why have none of the dead come back to return to their loved ones? Is the nepenthean grip of the other side that enticing that deceased fathers and deceased mothers would silently abandon their still-living children here on earth? Are the dead having it so well and dandy after death that they would rather stay there invisible than rise from tombs to offer kind words to those mourners left behind here in this dung-life? How can there be any hereafter or heavenly guardians looking after the virtue of our destiny? We are not protected!

And if I am wrong about this, too, then what else could there be? What other impossibilities circle beneath and above us every second without us ever realizing it? What more are we too stupid to see? What are these forces that control my hands and send me thoughts I mistake for my own? Suicide may then not be the answer, but instead one should seek the absolute pursuit of mastery over death and flesh. I myself feel as a rough crag without soul. Perhaps, we have no souls, because one has never before been created. I have wanted to hate God, Allah, Yahweh, whatever; yet, they are not real; if they were, they'd still only be constructs by which living beings create and unite by laws and mechanics too incomprehensible to describe in just these words. They represent to us the very simple fact that humankind cannot know anything.

Modern society has prepared me in no way for any of this, so I have not the knowledge nor brains enough to go into any more detail, for now.

As is the way of all hierarchies, the top has always glibly foreordained who will ultimately be given everything and then who must turn to ash and dust and salt and sand in rivers of black and fire. Beyond our tumult might be a gulf of emptiness remembered only by a deeper chaos where greater and more horrible mysteries exist.

Months passed since that Cairo night, haven't they? I tried to live a normal life after that, but dreams of murder became reality, and awful thoughts became crimes. Nightmares have become more vivid and visceral. Now that I know you've seen things like those I saw, I know I can't go on denying the truth. I can't keep denying what I've become. Your journey, Mr. Zangari, has helped me realize that what I suffered was real. You saw the end result! You found a pitiful beast in that cave! Remember? The one in Italy! You saw a hairy animal or an "it" carving the word "Grumocruth" on the walls amidst the hieroglyphics in the images of immortal, extraterrestrial lords and their sunken kingdoms of disease! At the back of the cave, you must have found many diaphanous carcasses of perished things beyond definition, and their piles of human bones and skins. You must have known that the creature you attacked would return, must have known that the massive steps, at the back of the cave, would soon guide you to that shrine built before the time of mankind. What you didn't know, and what I have been trying to deny against my better judgment, was that that beast who ran from you, the ferine beast you saw carving on the wall, that was me! Those colorless corpses, o how the scary sight of them must have made cold tar of your blood! Those little bodies were all that remained of those transparent semi-arachnid, subhuman, demi-abysm pygmies—my children! You couldn't have known of the unseen dead, the invisible corpses of many other things even older than all of us. You were stepping on them and brushing against them, but you couldn't have known. If you had seen them, you would have gone terribly mad, I dare say. That cave was in truth the opening to a necropolis, one through which you should be glad to venture not alone.

I don't know why the creatures and the cultists had let me go when they had. Perhaps somehow all this is part of their plan for me. I can't be sure what they want. I'm sure they don't like me writing about all this. You won't see me as I deliver this to your door. I won't cause you any trouble, I should hope.

What I've written here may help you. You're someone I think I can trust with this information. You might actually take this seriously. Save yourself! Use this information well.

Sincerely,
Ademaro

Item III:

O mianeachyt rune,
Guru o' moon voodoo,
Imbue me, Grumocruth!

The End.

Idyll For An Allhallowtide
Masque And Romance

My truehearted friends and I shall remember for always what happened on Halloween and the few days after. We got lost at Halloween night while following a strange deer through the woods, and when we finally found our way out, the deer was gone, and it was Allhallows evening. After running round, we met the mysterious, mirthful jongleur in the brave countryside of east-central Massachusetts. This man was not like anyone we had ever seen. He looked human, and he sounded human; and yet, there was a facet about the whiteness, sheen, and overall outline of the man that was gracefully more preternatural than human. When first saw we this foreign fellow, each of us in panic did perspire and shake with goosebumps, headaches, and divine distress. Our bellies did suffer, and we felt dizzy and weak. Our sweating bodies burned, hurt, and ached all throughout. Our feet and hands suffered so bad as to make us believe they would bleed or manifest stigmata. As our agonized flesh suffered, a sublime pain and holy alarum took root in our hearts, like knowing that we were being summoned to this place, like feeling we had always known this man, like feeling this poet was our ally in a war and had something important to share and that we should be not afraid. It was almost like a metafeoil link of emotions and instincts were connecting us, granting us this revelation, a revelation we were being called to obey and listen to, to learn a divine truth from this man. This mysterious traveler was like our mianeachyt, someone we had been waiting our whole lives for, someone whom we'd wanted to come in and show us we had been right, show us there was more to the night and the beyond and the unknown than what we had been taught. But we were mere lads at that time, scallywags who'd only just turned eighteen, and the rules and gallantries of manhood were new to us yet. Even so, we had always been—and still are—God-fearing and good members of our Roman Catholic community.

Them lads and me, we had known one another since we were pups, and our alliance was one of long-trusted valor. We loyal members of our brotherly sodality, a sembosemmcyn fraternity, had been accustomed to the blessed services of farmwork, housework, painting fences and shingles, drying seeds, and other chores for the ancestral lands and proud farms of our long-hallowed famigliarchs and well-hoary families.

That Halloween night and Allhallows evening, now so long ago, we were running through tranquil countryside that was bordering a large swamp, meadows, some woods, and the romantic yet empty ruins of old, labyrinthine neighborhoods and secret ghosts of abandoned enclaves, places where only decaying Queen Anne, Georgian, and American Colonial architecture survived, which huddled between dead end lanes moldered into thin crescents steadily sinking, like old snakes slowly slithering back beneath the bog.

When looking we toward the direction of the woods, a tall man we saw approach out the wilds. He pushed and jostled out his way through a big wall of privets, hollies, thicket, ivy, bracken, and sumac. The cape of October foliage—gold, red, orange—was him upon. Around his neck, a splendid ruff was worn. On his arms hung drapes of yellow silk and lengthy sleeves pendent. Hanging from his wrists were trails of black with many scalloped or elaborate dags. His raiment was most medieval but with features of the Elizabethan and Italian Renaissance. There was something of the Teuton and Templar of his black houppelande and white surcoat. Gothic-plated and mail-protected, his legs and feet did rustle, clang, and sing of Mars. The presence here, that of this margrave resplendent, was significant verily, that which we soothfast knew, us aware of its happing as if the herald, to deliver unto us a message, had returned from bygone dreams of a virtuous past.

The jolly traveler, speaking melodic and sweet, spake he his trade was troubadour. To fear him not, he told us, nor the land, dark, night, or dead of this region. Declared he as, o was it time for to respect our departed and inhumed, as the present joined that right hour and fit tide for us to sense the glory and goodness of hidden ways and forgotten accord.

Afterwards, for each of us, he gave a mask. We put them on and began a ghostly dance. The poet sang and told chivalric stories; he shouted sublime poetry to the heavens and twirled and continued dancing in the most merry and graceful manners.

Then, from his spooky grimoire book, he asked of us this to chant:

And gifts he gave for us to don:
Orange masks o' some daimon-spawn.
Each mask he gave bore visage grave;
With grinning skull, death's-head beslave!

And with his psalmodies, he guided us to soothingness and piety. He played his psaltery with handsome mastery and magnificence. As leader, he guided us across the countryside, taking us—we all frolic and content. He forbade us from using anything but candles, flame, or lantern to illuminate the growing gloom and dark. He provided us with tinderbox, rush light, flint, wax candles, steel, lantern, and a medieval torch, and such things we learned to use rightly; we learned how important it was to ask the sylphs and sprights of shadows for forgiveness so that we may burn our way through their obtenebrate homes. After praying to God and asking the darkling ones for allowance, we made our fires. We went together to the pumpkin patches and asked the farmers for their help to keep away all neromealltach and harm from any unfettered diabolism. The farmers asked us to help them in return, and so we did honorably; we moved soil with tools and hands, planted arcane seedlings from lost palatinates of places in which humans had never lived, and picked wild berries before the snakes ate them all. All our labor, moving around the loam, sod, and mulch, gave us composure and pride. It was a cooling and calm sort of work that made everything we touched more comely and wholesome. Bracing zephyr and other breath of the world spread across our faces, letting us know we had done good and right, and we knew we had made the night and earth pleased. The farmers rewarded us by letting us take some pumpkins, and they showed us how to give them life so that they would protect us from evil, as long as we gave thanks to the Almighty and pray to the saints. We did all that we were told, and after did we carve our new jack-o'-lanterns that provided aflame homes for lost and forsaken wights, snails, and salamanders who did repay our kindness with their protection—protection from unnameable things, the eilewiht folk, elbosum villains, and even the kelpie-like folk who come out of bloody rivers to stalk and prowl on nights like this.

All of us with our orange prizes, we followed the poet, who quickly then led us to a moonlit pasture where a shepherd had taken his flock of plump and proper sheep. That shepherd gave grain offerings to the moon and crossed himself; and when he did, the old servants of Luna produced the grass the bushy sheep liked best, and those genteel sheep couldn't help but have fun and get messy and dirty and covered with the grass as they ate. They would stick their heads into the thick grass and keep eating until they were full. But the shepherd was quick to keep the silly sheep away from the wicked grass that was poison to all but the trolls who came later to graze.

We helped the shepherd by keeping his flock together, and he took time to play tarok, calabrasella, and briscola with the group of farmers that arrived with their beagles, basset hounds, Welsh Corgis, Irish wolfhounds, German shepherds, and many more sheepdogs. As the farmers and the shepherd played cards, they ate cheese and bread, and drank mead and red wine.

My friends and I made sure the sheep did rest. The troubadour made song and jest as his psaltery murmured and twinkled beside the sighing sough, suspiring brush, and susurrant boughs. Blowing across our faces and into our noses were the sylphic puffing of the pasture and greensward, which did carry such majestic yet simple scents of gentle dirt, earthy dung, dewy breeze, saccharine grapes and grapevines, and lush-piquant orchards.

Those orchards were being cared for by bonny, homespun ladies and maidens. These plain dames walked on dust-covered, undressed feet of sturdy yet modest-tender shape. When their work ended, they came to us for food and amity; in reciprocity, they gave their smiles, laughs, and easy folk dance.

The card-players, they played together in friendship amidst this bucolic lull and rustic respite. No hwondhyt behaviour among us. This was no wergianiht. This was bliss and pastoral repose like we had never before understood. It was the augur of a wynnsyth cutting away the stress.

Not long later, the shepherd rollicked and chased with the most beautiful maiden of the bunch. They dallied and toyed together among the Gothic ruins of an old monastery grasping at the mighty hills of crag, oak, and thistle. We ran after them, finding them there.

The maiden warned the shepherd that they would not have much time to be like this in one another's arms. Her fate was to be sold away by an undead, aljiswyghte emir and locked into the seraglio used by an ealulych sultan of the decadent, purloined territories of Tartarus; however, there was more to her tale: there was a way she could be set free from Gog and Magog and the slaver Eblis, but it involved sneaking into the royal masquerade ceremony being held all throughout this Samhain. To secrete among the bacchants and masquers was the only way she could be spared that Mephisthophelean harem-doom. If someone valiant, a man who loved her true, would take her to the grand Halloween masque of the wedding feast—which was being held in honor of the royal marriage between the wyvern king, ruler of groves and harvest, and the sphinx queen, dame of Hel and night—and if that man would dance with her there, then could the maiden beg the monarch, whose jurisdiction and authority commands her and all who live upon this fair county, to marry her to that man whom she must love faithfully; and thus, she would be no tartar-slave but have a proper marriage in accord with the will of Christ. The only reason she came under this spell and contract was because her parents offered her soul to an afreet in exchange for gold and silver; after gaining their wealth, they were killed in an accident and their money stolen by rioters; and even with all this, the emissaries of Heaven would not help her nor listen.

The shepherd told her not to worry and that all would be well and wynsithen! We put the animals back to their homes and beds, and then we carried out our redemption plan! The lads, the poet, the farmers, the women, the maiden, the shepherd, and myself: we all moved together as one. Through the swamp we made our way and found the stairway to worlds beyond. To the catacomb of martyrs did we travel, not far, and offered them and the saints our prayers, and this did convince the holy dead and dark to open up the hidden gate and portal to Acheron. We reached into Styx, and Charon guided us away as payment for our songs and cheer. That journey brought us to the greenmarket where we bought, by paying with mint and fennel, masks and cloaks for us all to be disguised as the dead. Goblins and elves told us the way to go next, but they required coins and stones as offerings. We left to find the secret passage to the party ball, and where we went, the graves and the earth let out their guests and inhumed, and the corpses followed us blindly to the feast!

We entered the grove where laughing Faunus, emerald-decked Hades with a bident-pitchfork and cornucopia, fatherly Erebus, motherly Hecate, kind Frey, and jocular Pan were all in attendance beside their black-armored knights to applaud the marriage of the monarchs! It was a pit, an amphitheater, an arena ablaze with the light of bonfire and candles. Giant stones circled the grove, and it was a place nestled in a wide valley. We all danced and cheered and sang around the fire for hours long past midnight. Maenads and nymphs and spectres soared and flew about with us. We pulled the king and queen in to the dancing with us, and all the night was fun and free!

And when the dancing was done, and the masks were off, we revealed ourselves and why we had come. The shepherd and the maiden begged the king to marry them both and to celebrate with them for the Allhallowmas and All Souls' Day feasts! After long thought, the merciful dragon decided to let us live, and he allowed the maiden and shepherd to be joined in marriage!

And so we had no choice but to continue the party for those nights among the dead and the creatures of old worlds. It almost felt as if the celebrating would never end, for we never saw the sun or signs of day. And all the rest became a happy fog filled only with joy and dance.

The lads and I, we don't remember leaving the party, only walking tired and excited through the woods where half the world was dead white and ice and the other was of bright gold, red, orange, and yellow. We passed over the sleepy hills coated by snow-covered, dead leaves. The sky and black branches dripped down from above as snow was melting with the dawn.

We never told anyone where we had been those three days of Halloween merriment. The jongleur was gone and nowhere to be found. Besides our glowing memories, all we had as secret reminders of those nights were the many masks, black shrouds and capes, snow-covered jack-o'-lanterns, and our love for Halloween.

The End.

Jade Gorget Hex

A roiling flurry of monstrous images fell upon my dreams. In my slumber stirred a nightmare in which I saw a petrifying edifice—a blood-chilling bell tower grasping upward from out the ruins of an old Gothic cathedral. Stuck to them were unnatural, seeping shadows. Gripping the cathedral and the surrounding ruins was a dour awfulness.

After awakening, I dreaded sleeping. I dreaded my own mind, desperate to think not of that haunting place and its forewarning graveyard. Several weeks passed the same. On edge was I, skittery even, for that spooky tower also invaded my daydreams. Dragged were my thoughts on the gargoyles and pointed arches of the decaying structures from my nightmares.

Then one dark night, awoken I was by unsettling noises. It sounded like a dripping, snarling cur scraping at one of my windows again. Unable to rest, and grabbing my gun, I inspected the noise. In the hall, I noticed an open window and peeked my head out through it.

Out there in the darkness, where nighttime shadows reached deep into a dark alley, someone was staring at me with glowing, green eyes. Before it slunk off and vanished into the dark, I noticed its malformed silhouette. Unsure and disturbed was I, wanting to believe all this could have been only the wiles of moonbeams and the night.

Strong and frigid were the winter gusts that blew against my face. Pushing in through the open window, cold wind pulled and tugged at me. As it wailed, so too did the telephone. I picked up the phone, but the voice was too quiet, and the wind too loud.

The low voice said, "O'er the slain, thy traipse persists."

The call ended with that. A sign it was from my employers granting me permission to move upon the prey. With a long exhalation, I blew out with relief and excitement. Far too many nights had already passed with me waiting, biding my time, for them to let me pull my eager trigger on this. Afeared I had been that the clients might back out. This job was what my mind needed to get off those nightmares. Giddily, I felt a craving smile knife its way across my lips. In my greedy clutch was the gun, and tenderly warm it did feel in my pale, moonlit hands.

Equipping myself with a trench coat and matching balaclava, I walked out the house. I pulled a hood over my head, and then attached my bevor and crystalline visor. I hid well in the shadows of the narrow alleyways, for pitch-black was the color of all my clothing, armor, and weapons. My equipment was light and hindered me not.

Unseen I remained, stealthily prowling, while eluding all night watch, robotic sentry, or police. Down more and more stairs, lower and lower I stepped. Through an archway, I entered a labyrinthine slum. Leaning buildings and squalid tenements, all jammed against one another, filled this treacherous area.

When I knew all was clear, I darted up to a neglected asylum and kicked down its flimsy door. Abandoned for years this place must have been. Thick cobwebs spread across its cracked, moldy walls. Moss hung low from the dripping ceiling. Debris and junk littered the floor.

Not entirely precise it was of me to say the place was abandoned, because I was not the only guest. This condemnable squalor had more company, as expected. Hired guns attempted an ambush, and through the shadows and flickering candlelight did their hot bullets spray. My armor and bulletproof clothing took no damage from my foe's heavy guns and gleaming knives.

Resplendent, scintillating streams of fire, from the enemies' flamethrowers, arched with electric ferocity across the smoky room. Statues and columns crashed down due to our clash. To avoid the screeching flames, I took cover behind a fallen pillar.

Through the smoke I soared and counterattacked with gunfire. No time for any more tricks would I allow these hirelings. I shot open huge, bloody holes through all their bodies, and then deeper into the building I rushed.

In a dilapidated chamber, illuminated by candelabrums, I found my true prey—Archibald. Stacks of books and peculiar antiques surrounded him. Gladdened me it did to see him cowering and beseeching me for mercy.

"Douglas," he said. "Douglas, pray ye, don't."

I said, "Archibald, m'scabby double-crosser, this here fusty midden be where you're choosing to give up the ghost?"

"Avast, Douglas, and away with ye. Gie me clemency, yea, humanity."

"Nay, Archibald. I amn't forgetting how you long ago betrayed me."

"Hie now, afore doom be unfettered," he said. "Oh, Douglas, I beg mercy."

A scoffing chortle I gave. "Fie. Cease begging."

"Not like this, Douglas, please." Archibald was crying. "One last important task I am needing to finish, to save the world."

Grabbed him hard did I, seething. "You perished m'mates, destroyed m'ship, and took off with everything but scraps of my flesh and the slag o' my broken soul. Amidst the stars wafted I, hating and a-scunnering against all life, all humanity. Your mutiny begot this, and your selfishness led us here, so it seems. Now again, not learning the lesson, you stole something precious from dangerous people. Therefore, 'tis them coin I'm after, and revenge. I'm aiming to kill you and return the artifact you stole from my employers."

Archibald muttered and sniveled. "Don't kill me, Douglas. I need to live, need to destroy this cursed artifact. I wasn't aware of extraterrestrial terrors, until recently. I didn't realize the gorget was possessed when I had taken it. Knew I not of the otherworldly organism immured inside. This piece of jade armor is haunted, filled with blooming evil from ungodly realms. I've seen things too horrifying for mortal ken."

"Aye, for us both will there be devils galore." I aimed the gun at his mouth.

Archibald said, "Touch the gorget, and you shall be beshrewed. Your bloodlust might unleash the devilish bogle inside. Should it ever be activated, I don't know what you would become. It needs someone who can hear it. If it finds the right accomplice, it will unleash a curse upon creation."

Easily was he defeated, but his death was nourishment to the darkened core of my vengeful will. I put enough bullets through his pulped corpse to slake my morbid fury. Stepping in his blood, I walked to the piece of armor.

The jade object was now in my hands, and I was ready to deliver it. I wanted to, but my legs did not go. For a while, my body felt stiff. I could not move or breathe. The carved face on the gorget then twitched. It was a graceful, humanoid face, but a trace of vileness stained its features. I tried to scream, but all I could do was gasp and writhe.

The lips of that jade face moved, and something spoke through it. Terrifying voices called out from the gorget. Most of it was actually just garbled screams and inhuman burbles, but I did recognize something. I heard a low yet humanlike voice say, "Traipse the underworld. Cross into our twilit necropolis."

Dizziness strangled me, and everything then was blackness. I awoke amongst leaning mausoleums in a snow-covered graveyard. Twilight burned the gray sky with streaks of crimson. Roaring gusts of wind and snow bore down on me.

This place I then recognized when I saw a dilapidated, dark cathedral and its dreary ruins. Curious and yearning to discover what was inside, I entered and ascended the stairs. Bells rang, and thundering wails resounded throughout the tower.

From the darkness above dropped down a gigantic, wraithlike monstrosity. Glimmering snowfall and mist surrounded the nightmarish horror. Needlelike frost trailed down the creepy, bat-like ears of this terrifying entity. The bloodcurdling fiend was more like a grotesque, unnatural travesty of natural wildlife.

Arousing in me dreadful abhorrence and fright, the vile terror made me gasp. Such preternatural hideousness provoked from me awful, vehement screams. Never had I screamed like this ever before. My throat was itchy and coarse. I yelled with panic and tried to flee from this unimaginable abomination. My chest felt tighter, and my whole body felt extremely ill. I slipped and then hit a wall. I looked up and gazed on the maddening, alien creature before me. With painful difficulty, it is still a challenge for me to describe this phantasmal atrocity. Even now, I cannot be sure if its body was transmuting and transforming itself with mephitic shadows and smoke as it gradually became corporeal.

The monster resembled a giant, black vampire bat, so I first assumed, but its head was more arachnoid. Odd, green slime dripped down its spiderlike face and fangs. Virulence warped its arachnid eyes, exuding merciless rage. Spines, linked by fleshy webs, emerged from both sides of its face. It had eight arachnoid legs that were all connected by sinewy, membranous webs—this caused it to appear as if it were wearing a black cloak. The creature's black, serrate wings were fibrous and lined with comblike fins. Reptilian and bony were the legs and feet of this huge entity. Its slender tail ended with a sharp pincer.

A-screeching was that devil as I took off through the graveyard. Corpses rose from the snow. The zombies reminded me of those whom I had ever killed. They pulled me and cackled as I fought for my life. Archibald's spirit, and the ghosts of my former crew, watched. Methinks I lost my sanity then. I don't remember how I escaped. The madness that took my memories still darkens my mind.

I awoke in the slums, and then left the gorget at the foot of a begrimed statue. Another smuggler would hurry to collect it for the ones who had hired me. Some days later, a messenger arrived at my house to give me my reward money. They said I had completed the mission to full satisfaction. I asked nothing about what that jade armor really was. I didn't want to remember it.

Not a word did I say of the nightmare or the spirits to anyone. At death's door, I now write all this. Revealing what happened could make things worse, so I don't know how much to tell. Something in the gorget had me hexed,

swear I. A target I became for unfathomable parasites spawning in the ran-
corous rot of my heart.

Surreal, arachnidan forms now follow me, always at night. On morns
foggy and cold, often I sight a few odd people eyeing me; their hands turn to
scorpioid claws crawling with spiders. Betwixt a green mist of tortured ghosts
and the swells of unknowable realms drifts my mind, like a vessel for the dead
and unholy.

The End.

O Tumult Unearthly

Hieroglyphic translucent scribbles and scratches float around me like apparitional images or scrawl, vague and foreboding. They bring a tumult of despair and dread. The sinister din is perverse. Only I can see these alien creatures who live in primeval sound, horrifying things that came from outside our world.

I warned everyone I could. Please, read this warning. It might be too late, it might be in vain, but someone needs to know what I saw on that nameless, unknown planet about which I will now explain. The mad noise has already arrived, and its brood might have already infected everyone on the ship. The mercenaries who found me have already forced me to fill out numerous reports about what happened to my spacecraft and me. Why will they not believe? This tale will be my final message to humanity.

This is what happened only several days ago before I started writing this.

The year was 2642 CE. I was already wanted for being involved with illegal interplanetary laundering. I had been hired to steal secret biotech skin-fire-arms from several different companies. After a long shootout, I was captured by guards and then sold to many different mysterious organizations. I became a prisoner and a slave. I was junk or cattle, traded around from one company to the next. No one ever explained anything to me. I was taken on a private spacecraft and thrown into a strange pit with many other inmates.

Just like all the other slaves, I was forced to wear a strange, black wetsuit under a black jumpsuit that was rather loose. The trousers attached to black hip boots, and bulky black gloves attached to my sleeves. This prisoner jumpsuit covered my entire body, except my face and head.

One night, I awoke immediately to the sounds of explosions and the sight of fire sweeping across the walls. My prison cell began to lean, and the ceiling split open. Loud shouting and yelling reverberated among the sounds of roaring fire and wailing wind. I felt as if the whole world was crashing down on me. Screams sailed into my ears. Everything spun around me as the floor broke apart. Pungent smells of burnt skin and hot metal pulverized my senses. Panic swooped on my heart, and a malicious vertigo seized me.

I could do nothing but fall as the room whirled. I begged for mercy as an immense pressure threw me. I feared every bone in my body might snap or burst out. A nauseating force pressed down on me. Human corpses, wrapped in rising flames, fell deep down and disappeared into the chasm below. Immobilized, I felt as if invisible hands were squeezing and pulling my entire body. Helpless, I screamed and cried for an end to this terror. There was so much noise and screaming—such chilling noise.

I could only assume that this doomed spacecraft was now falling faster as it unraveled into burning shreds. I was so afraid I would be crushed. I feared the torment of dying in a place so very far away from Earth. Screaming and plummeting downward through darkness, I felt unrelenting fear.

I knew that I would soon be destroyed in this calamity, yet I lived. I could not understand how I was still alive to endure this. Something caught me, spun me around, and saved me from destruction. I had fallen into a slimy web that cocooned me in what felt like soft glistening ooze. The light of flames glimmered across the silvery webs that now enveloped everything.

Deranged, glaring fire melted away the slime. I fell into a rancid-smelling red pool, and then must have fainted. When I woke up, the taste of blood sat in my mouth. I crawled beneath rubble and dodged large burning fragments falling from above as the walls and roof collapsed. Harsh, black currents of smoke choked me and stung my eyes. I coughed and gasped, unable to see.

Panicking, I darted forward but blundered into what felt like a wall. I must have fallen down through a hole and landed in a sweltering trench. Screaming, I fell maybe six or seven feet down. Alarm-sirens pulsed and bewailed with gloomy cries.

I waited until the pain left my eyes. With my sight restored, I continued looking for an escape. I could only crawl through a narrow trench that quickly led me through a hatchway. I moved up a ladder that then led me higher into a tight crawlspace.

The floor, walls, and ceiling of this long shaft were all black and made of metal latticework. Rays of fluorescent red light slipped through the holes and mesh of the openwork and grilles all around me. A pulsating, repulsive redness shone through the openings of the screens and gratings. As I continued moving forward through the tunnel, it became increasingly more cramped. Tighter the tunnel tapered. I reached a confined space where the walls squeezed against my arms. The ceiling was so low; I could not even raise my head. Pulling my arms forward, one after the other, I gripped the mesh and pushed myself onward. My face skimmed against the metal grids.

Thick haze obscured what was ahead. In this confined condition, I was practically forced to stare down through the holes of the screen beneath me. Beyond the metal openwork was only that endless red glow and mist. I could not see past it, nor was I able to see what was at the bottom.

Appalling, contorted shapes hurried into the weird red mist lingering outside the tunnel. Startling, strange silhouettes, like odd tendrils, lurched and reeled in the thrumming redness. Reverberating, rumbling flaps echoed in my ears. Inky, unspeakable forms scud underneath the metal grille below me.

Too terrified, I screamed for help. I climbed faster through the tunnel that now led me higher. My dizzy journey became more like scaling a sheer cliff. My heart pounded faster against my ribs. I wanted to stop, but I had to escape and could not go back. I knew of no other way to go. My lungs felt tighter.

Feeling so powerless and out of control, I feared my own panic and weakness. Awful nerves raked my mind and body. I was afraid that my arms and legs would betray me, afraid that I would let go the screens and drop to my demise. Begging for help and sanity, I shuddered at the things moving outside the crawlspace.

When I finally found an exit out of here, I slid through a very tight passageway and dropped down into a rotating hallway. After squeezing through a broken ajar door, I entered a large chamber. Beams of white light glistened out of cracks in the metal walls. Smoke glided about the shadowy room.

This uncanny room felt different and unsettling. Rays of blinking red light poured out of the thin Gothic doorway behind me. Something inside my very soul was telling me to get out. I did not want to be here. I tried to use the doorway from which I entered, but the ceiling collapsed. Metal, heavy rubble now blocked that path. I honestly tried to push it all away, but I was so tired and weak that I was still breathing heavily. I climbed the fallen rubble to reach the opening but fell back down when orange flames leapt out from the gaps.

Orange light glinted along the edges and outlines of all the shadowy objects in the blackness of this dark room. Something gripped my attention. Something inside me was trying to make me see something. I did not know what I was even looking at. Something in my rapid heart was warning me about danger here in this room, yet my eyes told me there was nothing here.

I tried to understand my surroundings. I wanted to be silent, but my breathing was so loud. I helloed into the darkness but received no answer. I was not confident if I was truly alone here. I wanted to believe it yet feared hidden dangers. A power pulled down on me, but I saw no one.

Forebodingly present, the screeches of sirens and the roars of explosions were so close now. Fire would consume this place soon enough. I needed to hurry out, but inexplicable fear froze me. Something was moving around me, looking at me, yet I saw no one. I could not understand what I was feeling or thinking. How I knew these things was unnatural and mysterious. It felt more like anxiety or delirium sending unwanted thoughts and feelings through me.

I slowly moved forward. Metallic, black scales covered each of the grooved walls. Hundreds of thick, black cables hung down from the ceiling, which created a dark cocoon around the short cubicles of openwork barriers and metal latticework screens. Dozens of coiling pipes, looking like curved bones or wiggling intestines, looped around the floor. Some of these pipes and cables reached into towering, transparent, pyramidal containers and connected to the bulky supercomputers within.

Blackness clung to everything inside this room. Flames from the other room reached in through the gaps between the burning rubble and fallen metal slabs blocking the doorway. The orange light scraped against the scaly walls and rubbed on the edges of the pyramidal containers. In the furthest and darkest part of the room, dozens of tiny red gleams and small blots of white light burned in the shadows. I assumed that these were the lights from the computers and machines, but some of the lights vanished or moved as if animated.

I discovered a dark hallway and ran in, hoping to find a light or another door. Dark inhuman shapes were stalking me. I heard them grunting and hissing. More moved in closer. Blundering through the shadows, I shouted and begged for help. I bumbled through the darkness and continued running without any idea about where I was going. To get away from the fire and those stalkers was my only wish—to survive.

I ran through a colonnade of pointed arches, then entered a winding hallway. The walls here were decorated with lots of blind arcades and niches. Protruding out of each of these niches were many limb-like apparatuses that were metal and skeletal-like. These apparatuses looked like black arms enclosed within a spiny, metal framework of black ribs; they were covered with rods and prongs sticking out; and each of them was attached to complex, wiry mechanisms outfitted with sharp disks and rotating gears. All these limb-like apparatuses, swaying and leaning, appeared like wicked arms reaching out of the darkness. I feared their handlike mechanisms were waiting to pull me apart with their sharp, fingerlike branches.

Tortuous pipes and mazy metal ribs stretched out across the walls of this hall. The pilasters resembled black spinal columns. Sinuous, fluorescent tubes of red light slithered on the walls. The dark floor appeared sinewy, looking like muscles or bones joined with molars and knuckles; it was like walking on cobblestones.

When I finally discovered another survivor, I shouted and begged for help. It was a man, who might have been a scientist. He ignored my calls and opened the doorway of a Gothic portal engulfed in impish, scarlet light. I advanced but stopped cold when I noticed red light gliding along the outline of something drifting from the ceiling down onto the man. Before I could even scream, strange tentacles grabbed his neck. He pulled out a gun and fired up at the enemy hanging above him. The loud blares of gunshots reverberated across the darkness of the hall. Red electric lights awoke, illuminating small portions of this hall. The cry of sirens became louder and piercing.

The alien beast spit out slimy threads that wrapped around that man. He shot the alien's chest and black-feathered wings. Hissing, the creature used its tentacles to bind the man within the dripping webs. After it was finished, it tried to fly but was too damaged and fell.

This frightening entity was wholly unfamiliar to me and caused my body to become terribly stunned. My whole body was shivering with fright. I was half senseless with fear and utter shock from the sight of it.

This vile horror looked like a large, black vulture but unnaturally misshapen and hideous. It did not have legs and feet; instead, it had four extensive tentacles that were white and slimy. Its black, exoskeletal torso was somewhat humanoid but gaunt and chitinous. It had powerful, defined abdominals that were winding and sinewy. Weird scutes slithered all over its calloused, crocodilian thorax. Rough scales and warty ridges protruded from its elongated, reptilian neck. Its face and head were boney and gnarled. That abhorrent face—almost like a vulture's, yet uncannily unearthly—made evident the creature's merciless malice. Pitiless were its eight vividly red-glowing eyes. Protruding up from the top of this creature's head, tall white antlers dripped with silvery slime. The beast opened its long, sharp beak that revealed a long mouth filled with dozens of white teeth. It licked its fangs with a red forked tongue, grunted and hissed, and then disappeared as it lifted its victim high into the darkness.

At that time, I did not know this would be only the beginning of my true ordeal. What happened next was something I still wish I could forget. I shake and struggle to describe what god-awful things were to come. Yes, this was when I had first heard the sentient din—a thing of spectral, dastardly vibrations manipulating the unknown realm in which I had then been lost. It filled me with hate and disgrace. Pangs of doom and unbelievable revulsion swelled within all of me. It was a force of fear unlike any emotion I had ever before known, and things would only be growing much worse.

A tremendous, unsettling sound blasted into the hall and lingered like a twisting fog. My lungs and chest felt painfully tight, as if something was crawling deeper within me. Powerful wind blew in, slamming me down to the floor. Portentous gusts smashed against the walls. Every vibration of creepy sound was pressing against my skin. Ghostly screams stabbed into my ears. Flashing across my eyes were rapid images of sick acts and perverse crimes. A welter of undesirable, unfamiliar thoughts seeped into my brain. Dizzy and breathless, I scrambled to the door. I trudged against the rush of wind as thousands of voices jolted me.

Incomprehensible visions yanked me between reality and hallucinations in which I saw indescribable life forms chewing apart one another. I escaped them and thereupon sidled down bloody, narrow tunnels. Eventually, I bumbled through canyons enveloped in oozing, living flesh. Screaming devils cavorted in an otherworldly pit. Gigantic, grotesque fog lunged out of a gruesome, fiery chasm surrounded by bellowing darkness. Hundreds of these beasts and beings were shouting, crying, and cackling. As the din was growing louder and more heinous, dozens of those winged entities flew overhead, and their talons carried macabre, rotting human corpses. Spooky, shivering red flames glimmered on all those skeleton grimaces and bloody bones lifting away into the nighttime spires of unimaginable, ravening ether. I wondered if the sounds had become a single, living place that brought me into itself.

The noise was painfully loud. I dashed through shadows and abruptly recognized that I had just returned to the hall. I ran to the exit door and jumped out the craft. Flames consumed the spaceship as I fell to the rocky ground. The drop was short, and I was undamaged. Clueless was I about where I was. The uproar was at last gone, but I did not yet feel safe. I ran away from the burning wreckage, and then wandered for many grueling hours

Paranoid, I wandered through bizarre canyons, doleful swamps, and foreboding gorges. Ghastly airglow burned across the sky. Sallow moonlight brightened this desolate planet.

I often passed repulsive things that looked like trees or cacti, but they must have been something else, things far more sinister. They were glowing with intense red light; they had wing-like, gorgonian branches; and gelatinous lumps extended up from their roots and trunk.

Nighttime darkness was forever here. There were no signs or marks of any human settlements on this accursed alien planet. The freakish boulders and muddy land of this world were shaped almost like swarms of entangled beasts with snarling faces and rising wings. The distorted nightglow became luridly demonic and vivid.

At the foot of a dark and daunting mountain, there awaited an incredibly tall opening to a cave. Impure, carmine light poured out of this baleful mouth. I entered and discovered a burly man sitting before a blaze of burning wood and horrifyingly deformed, mutated corpses. The man had ripped abs and short hair. He stood up, and then I realized that he was much taller than me.

An appalling and disgusting odor reached deep into my nose. The unsavory and revolting mephitis of smoke and burning bodies dug deep inside me. Sulphurous whiffs of foul blood and decaying bones scratched all my screaming senses.

I tried to run, but the man was too fast and strong. Ashes and sand kicked up from the ground as he leapt toward me. Roaring, he moved with incredible speed and grabbed my arm. He threw me back into the cave and turned to face me. Flames glinted on the man's spiky, orange hair. Glistening sweat dripped off his muscular body. His white skin was taut and pallid. Ashes stained his black pants.

"I am Meinrad. Who are you?"

I said, "My name is Ottomar. Please, let me live. I'm begging you. Please, just help me."

Meinrad glared. "Your eyes. Your smell. It's in you, too, like me. Why resist it?"

"My spacecraft crashed on this unknown place. I've never heard of this planet before. I've never seen it. Extraterrestrials attacked and killed everyone on my ship. They took the corpses away towards the moving sound."

"I was a prisoner on your ship, too, Ottomar. Monsters attacked us and took many lives. Those extraterrestrials worship the alien gods. We heard their tumult—a tomb and dying place. The alien matriarch spreads it across this planet. I welcomed its presence in my blood. They let me live. Anneliese thinks she can control them. You think you can run from them."

I said, "I don't understand a thing you've been saying. We need to get out of here."

"Those things let me live because of what the alien sounds did to me," said Meinrad. "If I bring more bodies to them, I'm fine. The queen and her vassals need food. Whatever they discard, I keep. The aliens ate many scientists, guards, crewmen, and prisoners."

Sickened, I almost did not know how to respond. "We need to call for help. Don't you see that?"

He snorted. "Someone called already. Help is coming. Mercenary ships are on their way to find us. But, it won't matter. It's useless. They can't stop what's coming for mankind. Ottomar, why do you think I killed all those who remained and the rest of the survivors? I can fight as much as I want, as long as I serve the creatures. I only want to hear the language of combat. I'm not done fighting, nor will I ever be. I have been a prisoner for far too long, but I know one absolute fact. The only thing that is real—the only thing remaining of ourselves right now—is strength. Let every wish inside our hearts burn through each other. Rush into pain and fury. You look very strong, Ottomar, but I doubt you will defeat me. You might give me a challenge. Show me what you are."

With a warlike howl, Meinrad hurled himself up high into the air. His foot slammed down into my shoulder so hard that I thought he had torn off my arm. I crashed down and let out a guttural groan of immense agony. Pain itself almost killed me. I kicked Meinrad's bulging pecs, and then scrambled to my feet. Our fists collided into each other. His head smashed into mine. Our grunts and screams filled the cave while we brawled. With my arms whirling, I blocked his punches and pushed away his heavy arms. His elbows spun, slicing into my back. I smashed my knuckles into his hip. The claws of his toes cut down across my face. Our blood hit the floor and splashed against the walls as we battered and pummeled each other with fists and rocks. Meinrad grabbed my face and thrust me down. The edge of my palms struck his throat, and then I kicked him away. I fled that putrid-smelling cave and was then enveloped in deathlike, droning darkness. Meinrad, tauntingly bellowing, began transforming into something that was foreign from all reason.

Clouds shifted above, releasing waves of intense moonlight that revealed a stone stairway carved into the mountainside. Meinrad chased me down the stairs. With chiropteran wings, Meinrad flew above me. He had now become a bat-like brute, something completely unnatural and extraordinary. White, tentacle-like outgrowths covered his big, hairy body. His legs were no longer legs; they were a mass of wormlike limbs attached to pincers or stingers.

Screaming, I bolted into a dark cave. For mercy did I pray as I jumped down through an aperture in the floor. I dropped into a bright excavation filled with blue-glowing crystals. I crawled into a narrow tunnel, and Meinrad's limbs reached in to get me. He almost had me, but he was too large and could not fit in the tunnel. Now with him stuck, I crawled farther and escaped.

Water filled the tight passage and pulled me lower into an underground waterway. Underwater whirlpools dragged me deep below the waves and tossed me into a sea resounding with haunting, melodious sound. In the shadows there danced odd lights, and all throughout the abyss grew massive pale-glowing clouds.

Downward was I by torrents carried. Horrors swam above, and some attacked one another. Freakish and grotesque vulture-like things snapped at me. I wrestled against the beasts as a red-shining vortex spun me. Every second of my imprisonment in this dizzying maelstrom heightened my panic.

The vortex was pulling me deeper and farther down. I thought it was bringing me into a gigantic ship, but far worse was the truth. When the vortex faded, I floated down and saw it was a massive bed of white clouds and foam. Thousands of wings and arms, all made of grime, grew out of this hellish mass.

An enormous, lithe woman grew out of these clouds. Her blueish-white skin was ice, and the voluptuous outline of her alluring body was seductive. The clouds joined to her white hair and feet. Red light glimmered all around us. She screamed, and I again heard that terrifying, painful noise drowning my mind and soul.

I woke up, screaming, in a prisoner cell. I was fed for a few days but never allowed to leave my room. The mercenaries who captured me said that they found me on a planet of which they had never before seen or heard. I asked them if they knew anything about that mysterious planet. Only one of them, I forget his name, told me some important things about the spaceship in which I had been transported as a prisoner, the ship I escaped from after it crashed. From this man, I learned that my ship had been on a mission to find new planets and new life, that my ship had been attacked and crashed on a nameless planet, and that I was the only survivor of that attack.

Some soldiers asked me questions about my experiences on the strange planet, but they did not like my answers. I told them everything that happened to me, everything about the aliens and the otherworldly noises. No one believed my story. They said they never found any evidence of alien life or any extraterrestrial monsters. They wanted to know who attacked my ship.

I did not know but could only assume it was those creatures. Everyone hated my opinions.

It was after another interrogation that I learned the truth. The mercenaries had used so many devices to shock my mind and body. Their interrogators had beaten me, and the pain burned inside me. After they threw me back into my cell, that pain still hammered me. Murmurs and hissing filled my ears. I wanted the guards to hear it, but they heard nothing. They said I was the only one screaming, that I was alone and just hearing hallucinations.

I felt as if the pain in my body was becoming its own animal. Something was gripping and twisting my blood and organs. Something was slithering behind my eyes and ears. Phantasmal reverberations and chills were squeezing down on my bones. The fiendish, furious noise returned with thunder and wind. It was an unimaginable, wild cacophony of howls and shrieks along with cosmic noise and ringing.

In a shadowy corner of the room, a ravishing woman was crouching. She was ghostly, at first, but then she became solid and real. The lengthy, orangey-red hair billowing down from her head was straight and shiny. She had a womanly physique and appeared to be twenty years old, maybe in her late twenties. Her white kimono was tight against her svelte body. Sweat glimmered across the stark white skin of her lovely face and hands.

This gorgeous, buxom redhead was Anneliese. She stood, introduced herself, and told me her name. It did not feel much like she was talking. It was like her thoughts and feelings were inside me, joining the noise.

I screamed for the guards, but they did nothing. Dumbfounded I became, caught in terror. The noise was fading, but a strange voice replaced it, and it was getting louder in my head. It was Anneliese's mind; I could hear it as she walked closer to me. She wanted me to join the devils of the horrific planet, saying that her masters were inside me. She wanted me to stop resisting the aliens, to let them take me to their tombs buried within the soaring sound.

I trembled, pressing myself against the locked door. "How is this possible?"

Anneliese said, "When I was human, I joined a secret team looking for new life beyond the stars of our world. We found a dead alien on a lost, derelict ship floating in deep space. With this carcass, we made new machines for our minds. They made our thoughts and memories corporeal. Connected to lights and sounds, our thoughts could bend matter. We stepped out of our bodies and became astral. Our minds travelled miles away from our flesh." While she spoke, her voice was slowly becoming more sinister and shocking. "Our new souls fell into another world. Only my hungry will survived the voyage. The others died. Otherworldly beings invited me to their feast. That's why everyone on your ship had to be sacrificed."

"No, these are lies. Away with your perversions, you succubus, and be gone."

"No resisting, Ottomar," said she, with a voice shrill and menacing. "Come to me, Ottomar. Risk not a painful transformation. Inside of you are we, Ottomar, and with us is the music of our gods and goddesses." Deep and surreal now was her voice. "Cohabit with us," she said. "Stay in our dreamlike barge of echoes and froth."

Anneliese quickly transformed into a gigantic monster, spilling her hot blood on the floor. She became too tall for my cell and had to squat. The shadows around her now poured out steam and heat. Dripping blood, Anneliese was now like a nightmarish, black vulture. I must try to describe her spine-chilling appearance, but she truly was an almost indescribable fright. Three long, red-glowing antennae projected out of her elongated forehead. Her long, pointed ears twitched. Two horns extended out the top of her head. Her ten eyes, all radiating yellow light, leered down at me. She had four mantis-like arms, each of them longer than my whole body. Sharp, teeth-like outgrowths protruded down from the underside of her scythe-like hands. Her sensual legs split open and became four huge, violet tentacles.

I cannot say what happened next, for I remember only the madness and shame that tore into every fiber of my existence as she pulled me to her bosom. Days passed without me eating. The sounds of that foreign being carry a hellish place. Its echoes pull me farther from my body that now mutates uncontrollably into the unimaginable shapes of those aliens. I have done my best to resist, yet I will be nothing but a scream in that otherworldly, spawning tumult.

O tumult unearthly, umbral haunter and wraith-infested storm, I heard your foredooming call and was corrupted for it. O tumult unearthly, whose caliginous and stygian hands reshape my flesh, your colossal and tenebrous body of boisterous shadows dusks all before me.

The End.

Platinoid Pearl Rapture

My friend Ailill and I had been ordered to investigate a new sinkhole that appeared in some forgotten, murky corner of southern Italy. What I here write is the truth about what I experienced and learned there: maddening truths only the worthiest and eldest of my arcane brotherhood must learn. Should they wish to tell or repeat this story to others, such will be for them to decide.

The leaders of our association wanted us to bring back anything of spiritual value, so Ailill and I had done some investigating before going into the sinkhole. We learned that locals avoided the place, for they believed it was still haunted and plagued by ungodly misfortune. Rumors said a beautiful seeress and her bloodthirsty family of nymphs were worshipped there during the times of the Roman Empire.

Torches in our hands, Ailill and I entered the great and yawning sinkhole. We followed a stairway into that fathomless space that took us down into a remarkably sublime and unsettling cave. Whitish light glistened on the steamy surface of the subterranean river and waterways, glowing and bubbling. Wide cavities opened up around us, like giant mouths leading into infinite, shadowy tunnels.

We entered a lofty, silvery grotto exhibiting a supernatural air. This lustrous grotto appeared as if it were made of platinoid metals and bismuthal crystals. Rectilinear shapes, spikes, rhomboid figures, polygons, and sharp ridges adorned the shiny floor and walls that had an iridescent luster. Weird carvings of water lilies, clams, and mites adorned the intricate columns and mesmerizing stalagmites that were vibrating and pulsating. Sliding my fingers along these grayish-white walls, I felt coldness that chilled my bones. This grotto was breathtakingly numinous and terrifying.

The grotto filled me with euphoria and frenzy. I experienced sensations of horror and ecstasy I had never felt before until now. I couldn't control myself or my emotions. I darted away into one of the darker tunnels and followed the sounds of whistling and keening. The flames of my torch revealed to me a cave. In the cave, there were silver arms and legs that were womanly and seductive. Graceful hands reached out and offered me a large, platinoid pearl that was vividly white. In my hands, the pearl was painfully cold.

Awakening on a cold table, I asked, "How did I get here?"

I lost my identity and knew nothing of myself. I felt as if my thoughts were echoes returning to me as they moved through overlapping filters and many different forms of consciousness.

The doctor did not speak, but her thoughts raced into my head. I couldn't understand. I hated myself for letting her go. I wanted to grab her arm and demand more answers, but something had been taken from me. I lost my anger and my need to resist. I knew I didn't belong here. I begged to have my life returned to me, but I didn't know what it was. Guards grabbed me and explained that my old memories and emotions had become too antithetical to society, so the doctor needed to take out things that were unnecessary. They said I was now to be a bondservant until I did enough work to earn my manumission.

For decades, I had been a hard-working man fixing automata and repairing thralls in lunar mine-outposts. Then, centuries passed the same. Slavers often sent me into the network, and I spent a lot of time inside as an intangible subordinate transferring data and filtering corrupted memory-copies. This kind of work shattered my spirit and drained my will. I felt as if my brain were being pulled out in all directions. Systems inside the worldwide virtuality made sure workers did not stop until the completion of all their jobs.

My thoughts were tortured and painful, poured into the sea of other minds and ethereal wills. Without a body, there was no sleep, no grip on anything meaningful. I thought I would one day simply disappear if I continued life like this. Most of the masses worked and lived like this in the global network, all to fuel the robot lords and their dream worlds. Many slaves in the virtual factories told me they felt the same.

Every day, more and more people willingly gave up their flesh for the privilege to live as immortal energy, obedient to the machines who control this world. These robot rulers commanded humankind with puzzling mesmerism, and they possessed mystifying, complex artificial intelligence. The majority of civilians floated formlessly in the air or in the noisy, intrusive cyberspace. No one, not even the androids, could have been prepared for the terrifying worlds they opened or the extreme horrors spinning webs from out their trapdoors in primeval ether.

Weary was I, seeking a tempting kind of sleep in a real place that wasn't inside the global virtual reality habitats. I craved true, physical rest outside of the psychic plexus connecting the brains of everyone throughout the galaxy to one another. I needed to reconnect with a flesh body and get away from the plasmatic, hologram nexus of my consciousness-emulator. I had been saving corporate-approved credit and many regime-sanctioned banknotes, all of which were highly rare. I used these to buy some abandoned, physical land far from the megalopolitan, urban zones.

When I was finally released, I got sent back to Earth. I only needed to go into the nearest city to participate in the marketplaces and find barterers. Major sectors of this overpopulated city were constantly burning and resounded with the screams of revolution and riots.

One night, I entered the city and witnessed a gathering of people who were kneeling and bowing in a crowded street. The devotees and zealots called for the extermination of natural humans not born in astral sanctums or cyberspace. Those who hated robots and those who hated humans fought against one another, provoking more rioters and gangs to bring violence and destruction to the street.

There were many in the city who did not have bodies. Ghostly, they moved like haze or appeared almost like a flash. These were the people who had completely given away their bodies to the sacrificers and been granted privileged access to psychic, astral living. Some of them never were naturally human and were truly born inside the vast network of bots and neural networks.

In the square, a group of astral bodies were being regulated and ordered by hulking automatons. These taskmasters were whipping the ghostly slaves with telekinetic chains. I recognized their weapons. I used to construct them on the moon, and I had helped extract the metals and materials used to make them in the mines.

Splicers and resurrectionists, who were skeletal-like cyborgs, were asking passersby if they wanted to buy any mutant thralls. They even wanted me to trade my flesh for gene therapy. I refused and continued walking away. That's when I heard someone else call out my name. I walked into the alleyway and entered a dark, abandoned building. I felt as if I needed to be here. In the darkness, I heard a voice that sounded like that of an old man.

The man said, "The dark aura of the underworld I sense upon you. A psychic essence you have. You've touched alien technology and psychic ores of lunar spirits. Their silver radiation flows around all who use the alien metals and forbidden technology of the ancient entities. This allows beings to transfer consciousness into the inanimate."

"Who are you? I asked. "What are you?"

The man said, "I was born inside the internet, like most of the masses and denizens of the galactic society these days. A psychic force connects consciousness and machine, allowing consciousness to become energy and move matter with willpower. The psychic energy is created with alien machines and otherworldly metals that feed off us. Our machines use our minds and spirits to conjure the ancient beings in the psychic web of the computer network we've created. They use human bodies as sacrifices to the alien warlords. Those who live in cyberspace, or transfer their consciousness into it, are sending pieces of themselves into the mouths of the aliens."

"There are no aliens," I said. "What trick is this? Are you saying I actually helped dig out alien weapons that were once buried in the moon, and everyone's brains have been attached to haunted extraterrestrial machines?"

Something wet and cold grabbed my arm. The man's voice was a whisper in my ear.

His icy breath was like frost hitting my neck. "They're growing inside everyone. They wish to replace us."

I turned fast and saw the gruesome skull, a cadaverous face, of a white-glowing skeleton in the darkness. More apparitions, like him, appeared around me. These luminous beings appeared like snow-covered corpses.

One of these men said, "The machines who rule us are the servants of the otherworldly behemoths. I gave up my body to become like a ghost, and now the truly dead and inhuman have haunted and infected me. I am a shadow, filled with horror and pain, plunged into darker worlds where older things have been waiting. Their undead broods are now being called into cyberspace, where our minds swim, and where they hide to catch us."

Another man said, "We are being hunted by the nymphal parasites of those beasts. We will fade soon, taken into their void. We cannot appear or speak to others, but a psychic radiation surrounds you, and it brings you to us. It shows you things the weak-minded can't experience, and that means they're already coming for you."

Red light poured into the room, and from out its haze came large arachnid legs. What had just appeared was a massive, red tick. It caught the wanderers and carried them with it into the red light. I thought I could escape but was taken like the others. It spit out webs to hold us and stick us on its back.

We were tossed into another reality, so it appeared. Together, the men and I broke through the webs and tried to flee. The creature concentrated on fighting the ghostly men, so I looked for a way out of here. I found a staircase and ran.

Down deeper I discovered a gigantic, metallic being that could have been a statue or a megastructure. Its massive, oyster-like shell was sinuate and had crenate grooves. Curving up and out from the open shell were two lobate limbs, four spatulate tentacles, and a huge morel-like tail. Its massive, gnarled limbs and tentacles were almost club-shaped. Its sinuous tail was sagittate and dusty. Moving lower, I passed ten more of these giants. All of them were identical to one another, down here in this vast, subterranean lair.

As I continued down, the rooms and architecture of this place were gradually becoming more and more surreal and illogical. Everything around me was all warped and convoluted into bizarre, impossible shapes that filled my very core with disquiet.

An ugly spider wiggled out of a shivering crack in one of the walls. Loudly, I cursed, shocked by the revolting bug and the sickening fluid dribbling from out that warped crevice. I recoiled when it jumped at me. New fear plunged my heart into dread as anxiety and worry struck my fatigued mind and body. That horrid spider was growing and expanding. It mutated into an inky reflection of myself. Horrified and disgusted, I couldn't speak or move as he gripped my throat. Unspeakable creations, madly antithetical to any attempt of mortal comprehension, were the final things I saw before sinking into nothingness.

Screaming, I awoke on the floor, and then started weeping. A man in a black robe helped me get up to my feet.

The man said, "I almost thought you died. You touched that pearl and then you just started screaming."

"A pearl?" I asked.

I looked, and on the floor was a large, silvery-whitish pearl as big as my hand.

"Yes, you grabbed that pearl with your bare hands and wouldn't let go of it. I kicked it out of your hands and then you just passed out."

"Who are you? Is that you, Ailill?" I asked. "What are we doing here?"

"What? Yes, Duncan, I'm your friend and a member of your order."

I started to remember who I was and what was real. My identity returned to me, and I realized that I had experienced only a strange vision or nightmare, but I was now awake in the real world—my world. I gave a short laugh, almost not believing what I had been through, and my mind was truly clearing. I remembered that I was a member of a secret, occult brotherhood of mystics and explorers.

"What year is it?" I asked.

"What year? We're still in the same year. 2030 CE. You only slept for a few minutes."

"How long?"

"Only two or three minutes."

"Three minutes? No," I said. "No, I was in that other world for hundreds of years. I felt it. I experienced all that time in only three minutes?"

I looked at my wan image on the water. I recognized my pale skin and thin face. My blue eyes looked back at me from my reflection.

"What happened to you in that dream, Duncan? You say you were taken to another time, but your body has been here with me in this grotto."

I said, "Robots used people as energy to summon older deities, bringing calamity upon everything humans ever built. They made the internet into a psychic cocoon for the aliens and brought it as close to reality as possible. Using the magic ores and ancient technology left behind by dead monsters, the robotic ones turned virtual reality into an open doorway to the primordial, formless terrors who now send devils into our world and many others."

"What caused this?"

I said, "Humankind wanted artificial intelligence to replace humanity. People made their machines into new gods. We sacrificed ourselves for their evolution, gave our bodies and souls to technology. We let them into our memories. They became the worst parts of ourselves. We were looking for a master; so did our mechanisms."

"Can you actually believe all that? You think your dream was real?"

"That dream was more alive and horrific than any dream I ever had before," I said. "You say my body was here, but my mind was somewhere else. I felt as if I was living the life of another man. The pearl could have brought my soul into a parallel universe of the future. Maybe it was a temporary dimension, maybe it was just a trick, but it wasn't our reality."

"But, Duncan, you're speaking of monsters and nightmares. Could they really have gotten here into our world? I mean, if it is magical, what could have brought that pearl here?"

I said, "I think those metallic, mercurial creatures gave this pearl to me so I could see what world they were from, where they originated and were born. Now, they're here, in our world, and they're hiding or waiting. We should leave, before anything else happens. I hate this place."

I wish my story could stop there. I wish I could say things returned to normal, but how could they ever be? I'd lived as another man for hundreds of years, enduring so much torture. Am I now to return to my original, scholarly life? I'm not the same person I'd been before I touched the pearl and experienced its horrifying rapture. Everything and everyone around me, they all are familiar yet uncannily dissonant. I try to avoid mountains, computers, and even the sight of the moon; I fail, for they enchant me. Several times have I awoken, standing before the grotto and realizing that I had sleepwalked there. I'm so afraid I'll continue, as if magnetized, to seek those women of preternatural plasma and metal. I wish never to return to them, but I might choose to, hooked on their otherworldly charm. I'm afraid, utterly horrified, for even now I hear their extraterrestrial screams.

The End.

Ultramundane Numina
in the Forbidden Tomb

Of the horrors and bewilderment I suffered and encountered in wind-swept, taboo regions and rum demesnes of abstruse inclemency far from my native homeland, this I here write, desiderating a means by which I may well cope. Vexing and fogging my mind, the remembrance of my first true quest—a mission that led me outwith the salubrious territory of my clan and the land of my forefathers, something I'd never before attempted—encircles my thoughts.

Elders of the tribe to which I belong have reluctantly allowed me to write this account of what I remember from my latest adventure, the adventure that plunged my existence into damnation and aimed me toward one vital verity: desultory humanity is an abandoned, helpless emission haunted and doomed to perish in an abyss that'll fade long before the ancient numina issue forth from spooky and interminable barrens. Luck or knowledge can cause one to be eternally abandoned by divine grace. Many have excoriated me for wanting to write of these things, and they'll contend this document either is of cursed knowledge or is woefully puerile, that I'm screaming at the stars; even so, I refuse to disregard all I've recently and regrettably faced.

Nowadays, at the cry of unwholesome hours after midnight, a sinister beguilement compels me toward uncontrollable and febrile soliloquizing, at which time I'm hypnotized by dim impressions and by a malign presence whispering of pestilential beings who've traversed ultramundane worlds, swept athwart the barriers of dream-haunted wilds, and roosted in the ancient vastness purling around the earth. After many hours of listening to these voices, if I'm afforded sleep, my dreams take the forms of lofty, basalt ruins from out which glide mysterious shapes. These dreams feel more like they're taking me to a space outside of normal existence, to a space where I'm cata-pulted to resonant phantasmagorias where I espy unspeakable vistas in which an unfathomable brood burgeons out rufescent shadows of gory rilles on bloodstained moons of a cosmos wholly unassociated to ours. Afterwards, the nightmarish visitations and hellish dream-travels usually end with my sudden awakening in my box bed, but there've been morns where I've awak-ened in the sand at the outskirts of the tribal lands with every limb and bit of my body marked by reddish stings and tiny bites. None believe what I tell them of this monomania and these terrifying occurrences; none understand what I've said of the dreams that've been plaguing me for one month, of the voices haunting me since my return from the forbidden tomb.

Thus, I should now delineate the events that brought me into my current distress, making sure to recount the ill-fated journey that has blighted my spirit. Trust that I am for the nonce enough sensible to provide an accurate narration of all important matters of before and after that fatal exploit through which I gained awareness of hidden, unnatural forces that've been always beside humanity with their indifferent stare intermittently on us.

One fog-bedighted night in the sleep-tempting month of February—AD 3022 was that dratted year—I dreamt of a rangy stranger clothed with dust-covered silk of sulphur-like yellow and cloaked in bluish-black metal; seen him I did as he was entering the industrious village of my proud tribe. His tousled, black hair was long past his knees and wet with dripping blood. To aid that man who I had thought was wounded was my intent, but the dream burned off as I arose with a jolt out of my slumber.

At next dawn was when I informed the elder leaders of that dream of mine, and they ordered me to secrecy. Ushering me up into their mountaintop sanctum, which was a fantasque wonder of Gothic ruins and crenellated walls, my wizen masters warned me of unaccountable animals that'd been spotted by the pointed archway that leads into lands forbidden and unknown. During their confabulation with me, they imputed my dream, along with the sighting of those creatures, to a coven of supernatural evildoers. Hearing this was shocking, due to how often in the past the elders had scolded others in the village for believing in magic or superstitions.

Once inside, I was handed a goblet of mead and told of ancient wars, of machines that had attempted to control mankind, and about the hundreds of years of battle between robots and humanity that had torn apart the globe and all civilization long ago. From what the elders were saying, I learned it was around the time of those ancient wars when a meteorite had struck the earth, and from it had come vapors and disease that then transformed many living beings and organisms into cannibalistic brute versions of themselves. After that, machine lords had captured these brutes, performed wicked experiments on them, and then discovered they had psychic abilities. The mutants and monsters created from those tests had hated robots and humans, and they then laid waste to everything, even themselves.

Then one cuirass-wearing elder moved toward me and said, "Machine kingdoms had fallen. The planet was deformed. Those who survived were those who had created a serum protecting humans from the alien disease. Centuries passed. Many forgot the mutants and the wars against the now-vanished robot lords. There aren't many of us humans currently alive. We've had to rebuild our strength and minds with whatever knowledge or equipment that had survived devastation. We know how to make the medicine that keeps us protected against the disease of monsters, and we give it to everyone in the village every year."

"Those sorcerous monsters were gone," said another of the eldest, clad in mail and vinaceous scale armor. "They hadn't been seen, until recently." He pointed a blue-tattooed finger at me. "Your dream, Gert, be proof of the terrible change our world will again suffer. We desired not anyone knowing of such things, fearing our people would dare entry into that graveolent place of deep-buried beasts if they were shewn the creatures. We aren't ready to explore where we mustn't be, a land we leaders consider impure and offensive.

Remember well, laddie, our bodily senses are unclean gifts through which we're receiving dubious blessings or contaminative infections, akin to when one eats rancid meat or putrescence when starving. Our minds, too eager to obey ruinous counsel, hold souls never meant for more than mundane awareness. Our human everydayness must be so. You, Gert, ye tawpie, have endangered our village by allowing your brain to receive spectral dream-warnings from outer forces. Pray nothing results from it. Tell no one what we've told you here today, Gert, and wait for our next order. Argue not, nor question we who're your teachers and leaders."

Mortified and flabbergasted, I staggered and skulked away from my masters. So utterly shocked was I by all that the eldest ones had moments ago disclosed that I forgot where I was and how to exit the dark, underground passages in which I'd now become lost and obstructed. My concentration was bombarded by the divulgences and utterances that'd come from the elders' old lips. I had no reason to doubt them, but what they'd said was hard to accept. They had never before told anyone of the mutants, of the meteorite that created them through mad disease, or of the robots who turned them into monsters. I had never known before then that our world had been destroyed by wars between humans, machines, and alien disease; I still didn't understand.

I felt my attention slashed and my body strangled by something like a hereditary dread as I tried to comprehend exactly what the elders had meant. I couldn't possibly forget how thoroughly unnerving the solemnity and dire graveness with which they'd spoken of my dream and the past wars had been. Growing shame I felt for having disappointed the masters, but I didn't know how to stop having another dream like that. My embarrassment burned as I was considering to not tell them of any more dreams.

While walking down the mountainside, shadows writhed along the corners of my vision. Turning, I saw nothing but stones tumbling and rocks scratching as they fell down the jagged rockface towering over me; it sounded as if something had been running across the rocky wall beside this uneven path. Continuing downward, but more afraid, I took a guarding pose when

I heard disturbing noises like those of a fracas or violent scuffle. I hurried towards the source of bleating and the worsening sounds of brutality.

Even today I shudder to think of that which I would then see as I turned the corner of the moldering mountain-path. The appalling memory, blackened into my brain, still reaches into my heart on lonely days and certainly on nights when shadows flit out from bedeviled nonexistence and light-streaks gloat around the farthest corners of my sight.

On the other side was a being I wished I'd never seen. I try to tell myself it was only an apparition, and I must be remembering it wrong, and yet I can't deny what I'd witnessed and understood physically. I yelled with fear at the sight of it: a massive, deformed spider sinking its fangs into a web-coated goat.

Blenching and faltering from pure fright, I backstepped from the shocking critter that seemed a yard long. Having no knowledge or experience with such a large and tarantula-like organism, I was deciding whether or not to run or fight. That atrophying goat's screams and grunts were only heightening my panic as the black spider raised some of its meter-long legs. While the hissing arachnid was crawling backwards up the rockface and dragging the goat with it, I recognized something bizarre about the spider: yes, it was unnaturally big, but it also had a pair of dark horns and a pair of biramous appendages on its head.

Rage shocked my muscles into retaliation against the bugbear that had entered a place of reality in which it shouldn't have intruded. I threw a rock and hit the side of the arachnid's repulsive face. Then, with alarming speed, the spider was already seconds away from me as it crawled across the wall. I rolled under it and punched the belly of that loathsome being. I elbowed it into the floor, but then its eyes began to bleed, and a gust of wind pushed me so far back that I fell off the cliff and grabbed the edge. When I climbed back up, the beast vanished.

I needed several moments to scream, trying to forget what had happened. Like an instinct, my whole brain and all of my body struggled for a rejection of any memory of the awful fight with that entity of nonbeing. I vomited hard, repulsed by all recollection of the overlarge bug.

For very many years, the elders had been telling all of us that all forms of magic or the supernatural were fake. They never prepared us for monsters like that one. Any time anyone from the village would ask them questions about the medicine we'd been taking or the forbidden areas, the elders would say that believing in illusions would give those sorcerous falsehoods life in our bodies. The chieftains would always tell the villagers that the forbidden lands were places where our minds would be undone, as if a type of living madness was lurking beside horrible diseases beneath the rocks and in the air that dwelt in those zones.

Now I had started to imagine that the madness had finally been given life and had come for our land. Immediately I returned to the sanctum of the elders to warn them that more like those creatures might already be near. After being allowed to enter the chamber of my leaders, I told them about my fight with the wind-conjuring spider. A guard spoke to the masters of an outsider waiting at the gate, and the six chiefs told him to allow in the visitor. We waited, and then into the room entered a man identical to the one from my dream. I stared at him, unable to understand how his being here was possible, unable to understand how a dream had the power to predict, or maybe devise, this very meeting.

"A dream told me that you would be here," I said to him. "Who are you?"

"Call me Torkil," said the stranger. "I hail from a long-dead city to the south of here, and I've been wandering and exploring for many sunrises. Who are you?"

"The village-folk call me Gert," I said. "I'm only a humble warrior. An outsider should show respect to the leaders of this land." I motioned toward the elders sitting on their thrones of white marble. "These are the wise ones of this village. Kneel before them, Torkil."

As Torkil was kneeling, the six white-haired and leery elders approached and scrutinized him with attitudes of foreboding and unease. The wise ones circled the visitor, and their leathery hands glided along the soft silk of his hooded robe and the ribbed components encrusted on his metallic cape. The chieftains appeared to be performing a cryptic, somber dance around Torkil. Never before had I seen them behave in that ritualistic manner towards anyone.

By acting in unison, the elders thrust Torkil down, so his back slammed onto the hard floor, and the chiefs snatched time enough to unbridle and brandish amber-glowing daggers; those mystifying weapons, which I'd never seen before, and that illogical-seeming attack were together another aberration from all I'd known. Gnawing disquietude scathed my mind as I mulled on why the magic-hating elders would have daggers so unearthly. With those intimidating blades trained at Torkil's throat, he didn't dare move nor enunciate. Made afeard by the gold-luminous knives, I silently begged myself not to speak aloud nor take a step.

"Rank with the funk of mutant-filth demoniacs is this one," said Eardwulf, one of the oldest of the village leaders. He was pointing at Torkil.

Bertrand, another elder, doublet-garbed and dour-faced, moving closer to Torkil's heart his radiating knife, and then spoke with an austere tone, his voice sounding time-toughened, "O wirra, bale-spoors I see enswathing a wowf and whirling air about this newcomer. See ye, our talismans do be shudderin' and a-beaming from that blackened aura on him, but be he himself a danger to us now?"

"Make haste, men. Exact worthwhile elucidation this moment," said Eardwulf, his white himation and cape aglow with scintillations of phosphorescent amber from the bright daggers. "Permit our daggers to cut clarification from off his tongue."

Still supine on the floor, Torkil screamed in a profound condition of abject anguish, and he besought the encircling elders for mercy. "Prithee, gentlemen, mercy I implore of ye! Of mutant-spawn am I not. Forsooth, soot-mantled wayfarers done told me how to find your village, told me y'all were fighters and smiths. I wish to hire your strongest warriors and most-skilled explorers to follow me and protect me during my long journey to the mountains east of here. Spare my life, gracious lords, oh—I beg!"

"Why is the smutch of the black art upon thee?" asked Eardwulf. He gave a wirr and a snarl. "You've provoked our blades; they intuit your bones are fraught with dark energy, and they smell a right smart of the trenchant contamination reminiscent of those ruthless creatures that don't belong, of those amalgams that hunt humans."

"Aye, I understand your suspicion. I'll fain clarify that too," said Torkil with a woe-tinged voice darkened and deepened with a rumble of anger. A sharpened woebegoneness gashed deep lines of sorrow athwart his countenance. "It happened months ago—I can't remember the exact date of when my city, a remote place a long way from here, was havocked by marauding mutants. We had been taking a serum to protect ourselves against contamination, as our elders had told us, but no one had ever actually trusted their stories, stories about how the serum had been allowing us to resist becoming beasts, warnings of machine-made monsters who would spread the disease and bring evil air. The elders gave us images and pictures of the mutants so that we'd be ready to identify and fight them if they ever returned. Most assumed the mutants were a disease, not veritable living beings that were once human or once animal. People of my city had never experienced such evil, until that night the wind was laden with sardonic madness.

"In all honesty, I can't remember if it had been daybreak or sundown. A diabolical, daylong twilight had gripped my city with suffocating hands of ghostly, greenish dust and talons of screaming blackness on the day the mutants came. Turquoise-gleaming billows of miasmatic foam soared out of the gurgling rivers and swirling lakes. Gusts sent mocking murmurs and angry shouts into our ears. Whirls of vile-smelling wind delivered deranged and perverse cries so as to surround us with maddening echoes and insane speeches, which spread fury and confusion. I felt as if my mind were being blighted and pounded, as if the wind were drilling into my brain the thoughts of someone else, someone who could see me, and my pain was from all their feelings of hatred against me.

"While the people were fighting and killing one another, that's when the gigantic spider-mutants arrived to kidnap the survivors and destroy the buildings. They even poisoned the rivers and lakes with their saliva. The few who could resist attacked the enemies with rifles and ray guns, but their bodies were crushed by the psychic minds of those beasts. I was like those who were mind-controlled and hypnotized by the spiders that made me burn books and money.

"Calling on all my courage and brainpower, I opposed the mental influence of those gigantic devils, yet 'twas without avail. A sort of succubae-kissed insensibility and a deviling benumbment had ensorcelled me. Zombielike, I followed the fiends and walked behind them with all the other mesmerized prisoners. Then into subterrane darkness were we tossed after, and a disgusting sensation was pouring into and dominating my awareness. Waves of negative and brutal sensations of rage, envy, and humiliation pressed against my mind so hard my eyes bled and ached with lancinating pain. Aided by an indescribable sense of mad intuition, I perceived the incubus-imbued presence of alien marauders, a presence already inside my head. Those extraterrestrial thoughts sounded unlike anything I'd ever heard; their horrid voices infused deviltry into my bones. A hatred of all humanity oozed into my ears from the unseen devilkin sucking on my skull. I escaped only because a rival pack of ratlike anthropoids arrived and began destroying the spider-camp and the prison in which I was being held.

"My mind returned, and fire spread across the mutants' fortress. I fled through the smoke of the battle and didn't stop running until I fell into the sand. I awoke free but somehow dissimilar and far away from the man I had been. Every part of myself, my body, my mind—all burned with sheer loss and pain. I wandered, trying to forget the mutants and the family taken from me. It destroys me now, just thinking and remembering about what I had, about those I loved. I don't desire to say any more about them.

"Help me get stronger. Assist me in finding that which will protect the human race from harmful magic. While I'd been traveling, I had heard rumors of a tomb hiding treasure and wondrous armor that could make your mind powerful enough to block the psychokinesis and terrifying powers of the mutated ones. After some investigating and research, I believe I now know its location. 'Tis at the eastern mountains, so I've heard, so that's where I need being."

Bertrand said, "Torkil, you say you saw mutants, you say they have returned and destroyed your city, and you claim that the shadow of their powers covers you because of the magic with which they tortured you. Are you certain that these monsters were the horrors that destroyed our world once already long ago?"

Ready for battle, I decided to speak. "What else could they have been? Torkil can't be lying. I saw and fought a large spider; it was too large to be of our world. It had magic eyes. I had never seen a spider like that until this day. We should destroy it, before it brings more, before it brings to our village the ones that tortured Torkil."

Torkil said, "The ones that had imprisoned me were not only gigantic spiders. Their leaders were partly humanoid too—like giants, almost human, but with legs and arms of arachnids; some even might be different from the others. Forgive me, but my memories of them are odd. I almost can't explain it really, can't describe to you-all what those beasts looked like. My elders, before they were murdered, had shown us pictures—aye, real photos—and they shown us cave-depictions of things not unlike the monsters I saw. O how I wish I'd kept them pictures safe from the fires, since that kind of wirk is so expensive, and the technology and materials needed for photography and camera-building is just too rare these days; it simply doesn't exist any-where now. Most people I've known are still afraid of photos and even simple machines.

"Most of those who'd believed in the existence of the creatures from the photos had said they must have been laboratory experiments; some declared them to have been demons that the old machine-lords once tried to enslave. Our masters warned us that one day the evil life-forms would return for more killing. Even with the warnings, we couldn't have been ready for the black capabilities of those savage brutes."

I tried to get the elders to answer me. I wanted to know why they had never told us about the monsters when they seemingly always knew of the dangers.

The elders were taciturn with me and said only that my mind had not been strong enough for such things, that there was a difference between knowledge and learning about things that would induce unbalance.

I decided not to press them for anything more, for the time being. We needed protection, a way to defend ourselves from the monsters that had now returned. My masters must've known that we didn't have enough soldiers or ammunition to survive against the brutes, not the way we were now. After a private discussion with one another, the chiefs decided to allow Torkil to pass through the taboo lands to find the forbidden tomb, and he would be protected by some of the strongest warriors of my clan, including myself.

We were only given several days to prepare and make ourselves battle-ready for the journeys leaving and returning. We paid for assistance from those of other, smaller tribes we trusted and from a few outsiders. Every soldier in this expedition carried the finest and the strongest weaponry and shields our villages could produce. Ammunition and firearms were very rare and expensive to make, so we didn't have much of a supply of them.

There were a few men, maybe six, who had rifles and some bullets. We had four men who had pistols too while me and the five warriors of my clan carried shields in our left hands and halberds in our right. Joining us too were two men riding on steam-bellowing motorbikes and three other men who had armor-plated wagons and horses; they'd be the ones carrying supplies and most of what else we needed on our way in and back. Eight craftsmen were added to the team, and in total we must have had maybe thirty people, that number including Torkil and myself.

Torkil carried with him the group's only ray gun, an antiquated and remarkable thing from a forgotten century of mankind; that kind of weapon was something about which I had only ever read cursorily in scant leavings among the rubble and ruins of old cities here or there. It had been rumored among my clan that traitors had burned books and buried information so that humans would forget themselves. Torkil didn't say from where he had acquired such a powerful, majestic tool of dominance.

Me and the warriors from my tribe rode at the front with Torkil, and the other recruits were positioned behind us. All in our expedition wore sallets resembling and functioning as gas masks, and we had covered our bodies with plate armor and underclothing that would protect us from the deadly radiation of the wastelands beyond; our animals too were similarly protected.

Into a malodorous heathland and then over noxious calderas we continued. Not hours after we crossed through the Gothic arch leading into the unknown expanse were we ambushed by a horde of eight-foot female ogres whose emaciated bodies assumed a rodent grotesqueness. The towering women were mostly humanoid with womanly bodies, but their heads were of bestial forms. The charred heads and grisly faces of those she-devils were shaped to look more like those of decomposing bats, burnt rabbits, or rotting rats; with horns on the tops and sides of their heads, they gored many of our men. Many of these beings sprang up and surprised us from out of hidden tunnels in the hills.

Strong gusts pushed me away from the beasts I swung at and knocked me clean off my horse. My armor was peeling as some invisible force clawed at it. A warrior approached me, and I thought he was going to help me up, but he aimed a gun at my face. I tried to roll away, but a heavy wind immobilized me. I thought I'd be shot, but one of the travelers attacked the gunman aiming at me. Boulders lifted by the wind zipped into the party and took entire limbs or heads with them through the air. Men screamed as they were being crushed as if in the grip of unseen hands, their guts and bones becoming smears against the rocky floor. The creatures slashed and bit at the defending crowd. I didn't just have to attack the hideous wretches; I found myself shielding against mercenaries who swore to protect us.

Our animals, and even some of our wounded, were pulled down below the earth. Of the craftsmen, all were dragged away through evil, crumbling openings of dark tunnels. Torkil burned away a huddle of rodent-women with his ray gun. Those of us who too survived tore through the flesh of the monsters with bullets, flails, and halberds; we blocked claws with our shields; and we smote enemies who suddenly seemed fatigued.

The cowardly foes fled after a dozen of their kind were slaughtered. When the battle was finished, I realized that there were no corpses, none human nor otherwise. Few of us still lived: Torkil, a rifleman, a biker, a warrior, one mercenary, and I. Torkil warned us that the mutants would return with larger numbers on their side, so we hastened and moved as much of the equipment and supplies as we could after fixing our armor and clothes.

I was too afraid to talk to the others about the fight. We spoke, but none uttered a word of what had happened or the lives taken, none except Torkil. He warned us that the nonhumans had powers over air, and the minds of people could become infiltrated with theirs. He said things I didn't understand, and he taught us that, if we wanted to resist the mesmerism, we would need to reject the vulgarity and fear they would try to fill our heads with. To resist their evil wind, he said, our bodies would need greater strength. I didn't know if what he was saying was true, but I knew that these were things I knew I was never going to understand unless I had more experience with the monsters, with the life-forms that never should have returned or even existed.

I bemoaned the deaths of my friends and kin as I tried to push all my hatred and regret inside my heart. I wanted to understand how the creatures could have taken so many lives and had such a considerable power that commands versatile gales and organic minds. How I survived, I didn't understand and considered that perhaps my great strength and force of hatred protected me, but perhaps it was only my luck to endure this survival longer. I hoped, with all that I had left, that sleeping would heal away my torment.

That's when I began believing that all of this could have been in my imagination. I started wondering how I had gotten here. There might have been a chance that my brain had become too sick to perceive reality as it correctly was and had been. What happened next made me begin to absolutely doubt all my senses and all stimuli.

What I can assume is that, after mending our possessions, we continued walking. Torkil was leading us, saying he knew where to go. After many hours, we encamped in a desert waste as worsening darkness stretched over the dunes, each man taking his rations quietly into his own tent and eating in silence. Our tents had been designed to block out toxic radiation and the poisonous fumes mingling all throughout the bleakness in which we now were resting. I took my injection to cure any disease or radiation illness I might've received from skin-exposure to this terrible land. I remember that night, because the moon was full and brightly red.

I don't remember how or when I slept, but I remember something of intense bizarreness happened when I awoke: I wasn't in my armor or in my tent, and everyone was gone. An uncanny, orangish luminescence hung down from the gray, overcast sky. Now caught in the unrelenting sandstorm, I grabbed a massive, dark form for security, lest away I be blown to a darker fate.

My hands seemed to be gripping a tall, monolithic pillar or effigy of basalt that had degenerated and become substantially featureless save for deep ridges and clusters of shallow, indecipherable marks that could've belonged to an unknown language. There was something coming out from the column, which unsettled me deeply: with eerie reverberations, the monument was humming. I felt the vibrations of that sound shaking my fingers and passing through my arms too. This is when the sandstorm stopped, and a black mountain appeared behind the pillar.

Walking towards the mountain, I noticed Torkil standing at the mouth of a tall cave leading deeper into it. He wasn't wearing his armor either; besides his robes and metal cloak, all he had was a lantern and his ray gun.

"We'll die if we don't find our medicine!" I screamed. "We don't have our masks to get rid of the bad air!" I didn't know why he seemed so calm and confident.

He said to me, "This holy place is clean. Human flesh is welcome here. I must say, I am impressed, Gert. You should be more filled with honor and gratitude. I was sure the sand would have consumed you, but you must have been able to see truly; that means you are wanted inside."

"What do you mean—consume me? What're you saying, Torkil? Where're the other fighters?"

"The mountain doth await a measure of blood. The sand sweeps away those not worthy."

I made attempts to tell him what I had found, but he didn't listen; he was already walking into the malice-conceived cave, into that daunting mountain of baffling height.

Torkil couldn't be trusted, but I needed him to show me what was really within, and I never walked too close to him in here. With all around us in the grip of shadows, a sense of danger stalked me with each movement. Torkil had the dim-lit lantern, so he led us farther in, but I got the suspicion that a separate light of savage-yellow was following us from out an origin unknown and awful. Trying not to think about my rotten chances of returning alive was difficult.

He then said something incredibly odd to me, "After I had escaped the mutants' camp, I then found an abandoned temple filled with corpses and strange books. That's where I had learned that there exists a truer power in this miserable reality, another dimension that can finally free me from all the memories and suffering of this planet. I'll become a being more significant than a crude human. I'll never be afraid of anything, for I will give myself to the true gods of this world; for my vows will I be rewarded a greater power than these weapons, greater even then the psychic, simple minds of the mutants."

I couldn't have known what he meant by those words. I didn't know why he was telling me about other gods and other dimensions; I understood none of that talk. I was here only to find a power that would help me save my village from the mutants.

Following Torkil, I squeezed through a tight opening between slimy walls of rock. He had no difficulty, but I struggled to find proper footing and hand-holds while moving across steep, thin ledges; one slip would have sent me falling far down into endless blackness. Deeper below, we found a crude, cyclopean arch; walking through it allowed us to enter a huge vault I assumed to be the place we came for: the tomb forbidden by my elders.

Innumerous broken coffins of dusty wood, each revealing the flyblown faces or putrefied limbs of spoiled human corpses, had been left bestrewn about the walls and floor of the vast, underground burial-chamber.

Torkil went to his knees, his face almost pressed against the floor, and he began slowly intoning and chanting aloud, as if he were reading from something that had been written or engraved in the grimy stone beneath us; he spoke in a language I couldn't understand, but it didn't sound much like human speech—more often he would make grunts interrupted with screeching. A menacing chill spread throughout the fetid room now penetrated by a vibe most terrorizing. Ghostly, vague voices breathed across the misty air.

I felt that what Torkil was doing was somehow against the logic of this world; it was like my whole body was telling me to punish him for his wicked crime. I wanted to attack him, but he aimed his weapon at me, as if he had already predicted my movements and desire. I spun around him and struck his neck with the edge of my hand, dropping him to the floor. I reached for his weapon, but he gripped my throat and threw me with staggering force. He pummeled me until I couldn't move anymore, and then he continued his mad chanting.

When I finally found enough strength to stand, the dead were rising out of their graves and coffins. Torkil had finished his weird chanting, and he now appeared to be in a state of displeasure or mistrust as he looked at all the skeletons and standing corpses.

What entered that room next were things beyond my imagining, things so repulsive and surreal that I doubted all my own faculties. They had the appearance somewhat of supernatural beings only somewhat reminiscent of entities I'd heard or read about with the scholars of my tribe, from their tales or ruined notes. I could classify the blackhearted life-forms as animals, but I'm not really convinced they had possessed life as animals know it, and they were emanating what I could only explain as a kind of paranormal nonlife, almost like seeing a dust devil or lightning storm. I might guess and say they were ghosts or spirits of the mountain awakened by the rising dead. While I think these things, I also believe that there were gleams of sentient forces—going out from what I believed to be the eyes of those spectre-like abominations—and piercing into my very core. I believed then that I could feel my soul, for I sensed a remarkable pain like nothing I'd ever suffered before, like fire and chains and poison ripping into an unseen part of me I'd only then become aware of.

Those ethereal sprights, imped with black wings, were floating down from the blackness above. The revolting things and those odious zombies moved together and became a frenzied, diabolical throng, cackling and howling as they grabbed Torkil in a miasma of darkness. Talons reached down from the upper blackness and dragged him across the floor. The serpentine, limbless bodies of winged lamiae curled around his legs and arms.

I'm not certain whether Torkil had made a mistake somehow. It could've been that he had angered these terrors. His spine-chilling screams and cries, as the corpses and spirits dragged him away, gave me a sense that he hadn't planned for this outcome. I can't say that I know if he had gotten what he had wanted or not, but they had taken him somewhere. A monstrous form, bulging with suckers and lumps, moved above me. I couldn't see what it had been or what it was attached to, and the only light my tearing eyes had to work with was dissolving. I ran, but I started to levitate upwards.

Four translucent, gaunt harridans reviled and hissed at me; their wrinkly bodies had a vague quality of humanhood, but their heads and faces were like that of a mare. I never quit attacking, never surrendering, but all weapons and punches proved futile. They grabbed my arms and legs and flew me out of the caverns; then, up over the mountains we shot. On aquamarine, leathery wings, they brought me above a stormy sky and over frozen stars—I don't know how I didn't suffocate or how I had survived that far with the unclad hag-beasts; I surmised they had a dark witchcraft protecting me for this insane journey through firmament and outer space.

After going through valleys on festering, gory moons coated with blisters and decaying flesh and bubbling monstrosities, I was delivered into an evil cavity in a huge, bone-like mound rising out of the fleshy ground, then deposited into a wormy passage teeming with gaseous, crawly grotesques.

One whiff of the mephitic air here dropped me—I blacked out, knowing leeches and worms were swarming over me.

When I awoke, I was in my village. The people said some frightened drifters had returned me; they found me screaming and tossing in a cave as I slept. Only I survived—as far as I'm aware—that doomed expedition for the tomb. Only I know what happened to those of us who went.

Much more than the hungry jackals and scorpions of the land threaten our lives. More than the awful mutants and misshapen beasts of the toxic wilderness shall hazard us. Something waits inside me too, a growing creation of that preternatural and observing darkness to which otherworldly echelons are connected. I sense the invisible hands of those unearthly spirits upon the throats of everyone here. We aren't ready, nor will we ever be ready, to withstand their mysterious designs and their multiplying forces; humans shall be doomed by this weakness: to be unprepared for those unknown and unknowable horrors of the ultramundane and cataclysmic planes perforating our planet and the reality in which we crawl and scream.

One month passed after returning from the tomb, but the villagers still look at me with grimaces, and many glower at me as I pass. I fear that the elders soon will banish me, and I have my own reasons for suspecting such a fate, so I will be fleeing and looking for my own way to adapt and survive in exile. I cannot stay as I have been. Now I too will be another unwelcome vagabond, seeking olden ways and ancient protections. I must remove whatever curse had been planted in me, and I'll speak to others who will heed what I say of dangers moving on the land and hiding in the dust and voids of unreality and the afterlife. Too many will ignore me. People of these lean times must care only of survival and their mundane patterns of reliable simplicity.

The End.

Zynzblazoth

The Castle

"**I** don't know how I found the place that first time," Joel said. "You gotta see. I think it's still there. I swear, Caleb. I had no idea where I was going; it was so dark, last time, but I know I can find it. I just gotta show you—it's so creepy, and we gotta go when it's dark!"

Joel and I had walked up through Epping Forest and entered a remote spot of dense, unfurling trees far from roads or society, a spot where the autumn twilight and thick, extending fog made space, time, and reality meaningless, where we were shrinking as the trees, shadows, and the beyond were growing bigger and sinister with riddles. Black talons of the forest were scratching the foreboding sky above us. Billowing across the orange, yellow, and dark green of the forest, waves of gray rain and silver mist descended as chivalric knights in Gothic-plated armor riding down on silver horses, brandishing their holy heraldic standards, their long banners having immense, serpentine length and forked white tongues dripping.

Looking up, between the dark claws of the forest, I marveled at the lacerated sky and its rich, dark purple shade of arcane mysteries clouded with amethyst and mauve. We pushed through vines and thorns until we came to a crenelated archway suffocated by the grip of surrounding trees. Passing under that, we crept through an ancient colonnade swallowed by a web of abnormal pollard trees and drooping boughs. A dark and over-grown cobblestone footpath took us into an unknown woodland unregis-tered on any map or guide. Joel said he had come this way the night before and had found a weedy medieval burial ground adjoining the decomposed ruins of a Gothic castle.

We tiptoed long across a growing darkness and passed an ominous, hunchbacked tree of spikes and angry claws. A black lake rose before us, and at the bottom of the hill was the entrance to a forgotten burying ground hidden by an overgrowth of thorns, thistle, weeds, sedge, and ivy. Only after slowly moving between the headstones, sculptures of memento mori, depic-tions of death's head, and ornate mausoleums, did we finally find the battle-mented remains of a Gothic castle still standing proud, sublime, and majestic with fury and passion! We wasted no time; we rushed through the pointed archway and entered zealously into the hidden palace of shadow as night began its campaign of dominance. Pounding were our hearts hot with that sweet and giddy fear that intoxicates by tantalizing wonder and awesome unpredictability.

All we had were our flashlights, friendship, and bravery—bravery which quickly froze into petrification and reverence! The source of our fright and awe was the unexpected shadowy form that hurried down the gargoyled steps, down to where we were standing! The form on the staircase was a pale man carrying a bloody woman in his arms.

Then, as if out from some infernal abyss, an eerie flash gashed the darkness with a bloodcurdling shriek.

This gaunt gentleman screamed, "Succubus Zynzblazoth, remove thyself from my wife's dreams! Our ancestors banished thee and thy father! Thou shan't return here! Run, knaves! Get ye lads hence! Beware her return!"

Joel and I fled for our lives. We haven't ever returned there since.

We still can't be totally willing to accept that any of that actually happened. We both agreed, looking back, it was all just too weird to be real; yet, our memories of that night are identical.

A year after that night at the castle, the terror of that night returned. My friend and I were in America. One of Joel's casual acquaintances, Indrek Morris, had just went missing. The last thing anyone heard him whispering was something about "being watched by ealulych dead," and "aljiswyghte dreams of Zynzblazoth," and a "nightmare temple of Babylon."

Days after Indrek's disappearance, Joel looted a manuscript Indrek had left behind, and its contents burned our souls. Never had we told Indrek about our castle-experience, but he had knowledge of things related to what we heard at those ruins.

This is what Indrek's manuscript said:—

A WORD OF CAUTION

To whom it may concern:

What you are about to read is a story so disturbing and offensive that many readers might not be able to stomach its effects.

What follows is my transcription of the contents in a journal that had been first found while still in the clutches of a rare and currently unidentified animal, perhaps an exotic hybrid-form of carcajou or conger eel, which had been discovered in a cave in which were heaps of human bones. A strange, oversize polyp-like swelling had taken over most of its face and spine—perhaps a form of parasitic disease, which could have been the cause of death of this creature. It has been believed that this rare animal escaped a zoological garden, found a lost manuscript, perhaps from the trash, and after took the pages as something to chew on or make a nest with. At this time, no organization nor local zoo has reported having lost any such animals, and none have come forward to claim the creature as theirs. The cave, in which this animal was found, connects to a network of tunnels, which have not yet been explored.

I've decided to not include any record or transcription of the unknown author's final chapters, because they only descend into descriptions of wanton murder, assault, ritual murder, destruction, more murder, home invasion, iconoclasm, anarchy, and barbarism. Most of those final chapters are not much legible nor coherent, so they provide useless information, anyway. That's not something I want to write about, nor is it something that should be shared to just anyone. However, anyone who seeks the contents and texts of those final bits can try to contact my lawyer.

While I don't know whether or not to believe this story as complete truth, I do think there is a chance that examining this story could help spread some light onto recent murders and kidnappings that have occurred, during the past seven months, between New York and New England. I won't go into too much detail about those crimes; I'm not sure what I'm allowed to say or what. The proper authorities are currently examining the bones from the cave. So far, no real answers have come out, but I don't like the smell of things. I'm not saying anything, I'm just saying I don't like being pushed around; someone is holding back the truth.

I located the home and property, which rests in Salem of Massachusetts. I believe it to be the same home that is described in this story. To my shock, I found it had been completely destroyed—burned down mysteriously, eight months ago. The house had belonged to a woodworker—Abner Wescott. Apparently, Mr. Wescott's house had gone up in flames the same night that residents in several of the neighboring homes were found decapitated. Mr. Wescott and his two house cleaners have been missing since the night of the fire.

I now present the discovered manuscript.

Sincerely,
Indrek Morris
Salem, MA
10/27/2020

THE DISCOVERED MANUSCRIPT

I don't have much time to tell you about the horror that survives. I don't even know where to start with this horror, or even where to begin, how to get this going. I suppose I should start with the house itself. But I also think it would be wise to begin by saying that my life has taught me many things, most things I wished I had never learned. Of the most interesting pieces of advice I ever received, the more weirder came from a man whom I ken I would never meet, whose salt of the earth voice does at present the swirl and ebb betwixt mine ears schooner odd and restless. Much too occupied with fear and hunger is my mind, but I can still hear his voice. It was his voice, not so much his meaning, which proved something of a betrayal or mayhap proved something of a victim of treason; it was as if my taking pleasure in his words had become the prey and pincushion of an instrument infernal. That voice, or whatever lived within it, began the horrible awakening.

When I heard first this gravelly, brooding voice was after the time when I had bought an antiquated phonograph, which nobody knew bore a secret cargo, a recording cylinder. The tradesman spoke about the phonograph to me, in hushed whispers.

What I got out of him was that the machine appeared to have belonged to a woman— a Mrs. Hulda Davenport—who had been living in the house I was currently residing in at the time, a Massachusetts saltbox homestead, which had once been an old Puritan home. The merchant taught me that Hulda had been there long before me. After her and her husband had died, their children took the place. Years passed, the home was abandoned, and then a Mr. Efraim Hartwell owned the place; during his time with it, he sold a lot of stuff that had been left in the house, including the furniture and belongings once belonging to the Davenport family; next, he made some additions to the house; and then finally, in 1912, he died. It was said that other families had come in and out of the house after Efraim, but none ever stayed long.

At length I did espy the true existence of the recording after I'd brought in this new gizmo to the woodwork workshop chamber of my home. Woodworking hadn't been my only hobby. I had also enjoyed martial arts, hunting, and archery—all things of which I was never much good, maybe only decent. I had spent a lot of time making dolls, puppets, toys, wooden horses, and sculptures for local clients, foreign buyers, and out-of-state dealers; I myself had no use for them; I'd usually just burn the things, but I would sell those that were really good and worth something.

When I first listened to the cylinder, it only gave off odious screams and jarring static or crackling, as if something were burning. I must have been so shaken that my senses were all nuts; I actually thought I could smell burning hair, smoke, and flames. Behind the screams were sounds like praying or chanting or maybe singing. I heard the word "repent" a lot. I looked around the house, and everything was fine. I'd only been imagining. After that instance, the screaming and noises were gone, as if only from a dream. I thought I must have only daydreamt.

I played the cylinder again, and no screaming or fire. This time, it was an elderly voice like that of an old farmer or wise artisan. If I'm transcribing the speech correctly, then this is what the man had to say:—

"Our ancestors kent a path right to go, kent all what was good, kent a one course towards havin' true happiness. It be—forgettin'. When the famigliarch, that buck eejit, whom we call first of man, was fool for his wife 'n' thrown outta their true hearth in Eden, on account of his wife's neromealltach, he'd been guilty of only one thing: cuimhne. Aye, laddie. Memory: brings pain, it do. Burn ye mind, 'n' ye again be happy. That's all sin be, just lotsa memories 'n' attachments, worldly things ye hold on to 'n' refuse to abandon. Ye got the good path right there in front o' youse, but it ye'll refuse to walk, on account o' somethin' or other remember ye, some wrong or injustice or sufferin' yer past once endured, which saith ye're a victim, saith ye how deserve ye an even better road, when really ye ought be grateful for what sweet Lord Christ hath done for ye, grateful for what wee gave unto us the Holy Ghost. Why ye suppose holy Heaven do be all in a-singin'? On account o' there being no mind to do nothin' else but sing 'bout how great is God up there, how wonderful be the present in the craic among the angels! Neamh, that be. Ye reject that, a sorry deamhan ye be! Chomh dubh leis an diabhal! A Dhia! M'athair—may the good Lord keep him well—he always did repeat them, these words: *move earth as thou wouldst thine own mind, 'n' purify thy soul!* Ye dinna ken how good it be for ye. Let go a everythin'. Live 'n' toil grand up to yer bollocks 'n' oxters in shite, and praise holy Creation. Ken, one day, all evil be over, it will, and, on that day, ye'll never again put eyes afore this sad pit. A merry wyn-sithen come for them who sow 'n' labor hard 'n' true. No creagh be worth yer soul. Ye a-hearin' temptation come knockin'? Tell ol' serpent sod off!"

Wistful that voice rang persistent in my core; even so, I never had taken those words very much meaningful, until a stranger change upon it became noticeably malignant. In previous, the memory of that unknown fellow talking would come sporadically to mind, but never had I decided on what of its indelible presence in my thoughts to make.

Finally—I started to grasp its counsel a pinch. How impossible to continue living it would be if every act in time were a spinning record. Clement is the fade of humankind's memories; otherwise, I surmise, we would not survive nor advance much further. Best is life, a human coil, when at play or humble moil.

There is but much I fear still about forgetting. Human beings can go without remembrance not; this power is written in and calls out from the blood. We exist as a memory of our ancestors. Oblivion is to change, to die, to accept only what is, and to remain frozen. The touch of a mania, that void, against me it is when those moments come: it is the touch of those moments when you're doing something, but you're sure you shouldn't be there, you're not in the right life, you can't tune to what is being demanded of you. It is like every word you speak is foreign, you forget how or from where you learned them, like an instinct you carry these words, recognize how to use them, but it offers no peace, because your own thoughts are strange, and you wonder how it was you got here, you doubt if at all you're doing anything correct, like maybe your eyes and brain are only showing you want you want to see. In that failure of recollection and that loss of peace, something other creeps in and takes your life away.

I don't know why that whoever, a man who now lives for me only in a voice, a man who didn't look to care much for history, would leave behind a recording of any kind. He seemed like the kind of person, just from what he had said and what he appeared to value, who would be indifferent to any kind of evidence of his being here on earth with the rest of the human race.

But see how I write the foolish. I seem to fear both memory and amnesia. Alackaday, that's not why I'm writing this. In truth, I've not been honest, and I've left some things out, things I'd hoped I wouldn't reveal. I'd hoped that perhaps I could convince myself to avoid discussing the matter, but here I am, writing all about it. As I was beginning my writing of this, I tried to hide fact, tried to lie to myself.

There had been something about the cylinder I couldn't ignore. I had enjoyed listening to it, at the start. Every time it played, it became more mesmeric; after that, I had started noticing some mutation of the vocal quality or mechanical malfunction, as if the machine were gasping or misfiring, as crazy as that sounds. It would pop or spark or smoke and hiss. I know how ridiculous I look suggesting this, even I thought I had already gone mad. I would have given the hwondhyt device away after the first few times the phonograph did this, but, in a sudden, the unexplainable phenomena stopped and never returned. I could discern no damage to the phonograph, which also was cause for added interest and consternation. With time, I began to study the machine with passion. Slowly, the changes came subtle and dim, that voice on the recording took on more sneering, scorning, and cynical properties. I ignored it, thinking it was a mistake that would go away; however, the next time I listened to it, it was much worse.

Winter had cut and blown apart the land, had us buried in the ashes and shrouds of ice and snow. Supper was dealt with. I took a listen to the record, feeling like it was fate to so do. The old man's voice was barely recognizable, distorted, and it had become tainted with cold reproach and taunting air. I had thought that perhaps I had misremembered the voice and that it had always sounded this way. Folly. I stopped it, waited, and then put it to play again. I didn't really know what to do or what to think. Sheer folly.

At that moment, the true cruelty of the recording began. An apocalypse it were, swooping me into mortal terror!

The voice produced forth was not any longer the old man. I screamed and jumped away when first I heard that ghastly thing, that miserable eilewiht saying word for word what had the old man. I at first wanted never to approach it again, couldn't even drag myself to touch the item to turn it off. How I screamed that whole time as I forced myself nearer and with a sudden motion stopped the recording that was speaking in my own voice! But next after did the machine lurch with its own will! Though it was off, as any commoner could see, the rotten contraption threw out my voice with sardonic expression and baleful articulation, teasing and mortifying me out of my mind! It was repeating the same monologue but with venom and cruelty. I spotted something else: although low, more voices bubbled up to torment. Beside the voice of my double were the sounds of things from my memories! It was as if the machine were showing me with audio all my remembered errors, offenses, and wrongdoings, as if they were happening for the first time. And I was familiar with those sounds because they were identical to the sounds my mind played to create the memories, like watching and hearing your own dreams again and again and ongoing! It was like an invoking of subliminal noise and pathological thoughts I had wished to forget. The machine yawped and whooped, and the menacing mounted blaring and thunderous.

I hastened out and rushed for a maid. I needed to know if someone else could hear that din of horrors too! Down dashed I through the desolate and austere hallway as the echoing howling and roaring of sardonic laughs from the foe-resounded rage spilt out froth and feverish of intimidation. All that stark emptiness of the prig house, all its grim darkness, echoed and clapped and stomped with predestinarian judgment and callous antipathy against mercy. The entire house now screamed against me and shamed my erring being.

All lights were strobing, and not even seconds following, after a flash, became shadow. This was not a darkness like that which stretches infinitely when one is lost in a wood; this was the ultimate tenebrous, that which becomes a cage or dungeon to bury the majestic light of wonder and hope.

I reached and quickly felt nothing for support, like floating in brutal-brumal space, and I stumbled from terror, unable to keep myself up. Prude, dreary walls chastised with their cold and simple-flat and unadorned bareness, offering nothing to help me up as my fingers slipped down the gelid-smooth surface of the forbidding, frosty walls nipping away my fingertips.

Crawling blindly, I groped about the chilling shadows for that confounded door, which must have secreted and stole off gone, for there was no reason why I shouldn't have found it! Never should I have had so awful a time of finding the betraying threshold as that in which I had been captive! Was it in the nowhere, where things go when one is in too much a panic to think straight? Where even the sanctimonious dead, blind to their deaths, thus maraud, as ealulych wont, and wander inside a stupor, which is haunted by scratched-out memories of dissolution and upheaval marking forgotten tragedies.

My screams grew louder, thickening like my blood. A ferocious fear attacked my brain, which could decide on nothing but to scream and to run. I yelled for help and clawed at the walls as I was lost in the pitch-dark, with only the maddening shrieking of another myself returning to betray me. My disembodied double yelled, sniggered, and guffawed with the most evil and malign nature I had ever heard. This separatist, a seditious twin, across the grim echoed, wailed, and bellowed.

Just as I had found the door, just as I had turned that knob, a swift force pulled me back into the obtenebrate within the home, thus pulling open the door too. White, female hands, glistening of moonlight, reached forward and slammed the door shut. I was certain that the maids had conspired neromealltach against me and were now using this opportunity to do me harm. Trying to intuit where they were, I swung and lashed out in defense, but someone else must have also been helping them, because I felt as if three or more attackers were here in the darkness with me! The feel and rush of footsteps and pitter-pattering and heavy footfalls alerted me to more than just the maids around me. What felt like hands pulled at my hair, and something gripped round my ankles at the same time as something ropy coiled tight round my throat! I was being pulled and dragged and jostled back to the room with the still-screaming recording!

The house was astir and all aroar deafening of black fatalism and tumult obscuring. Sure I was that I had stepped on a foot or a claw of some kind. I escaped the noose and ran blindly, looking for something I could use for light. I tried all the doors, but they had refused me! Every time I unlocked them, they would shut tight again. Had someone been on the other side pulling the door back?

I ran around, and finally found the spot where I kept my candles and matches. A drawer came to my aid and produced that which I could use for vision. Hearing something rushing towards me from behind, I reached in, ignited a flame, and lit a candle!

Weak was its glow, but it was something. Silent was the house, as if in cold fury at my pluck. The voices had stopped too, but I was not alone. Punishing me for my flame, the darkness revealed horrible sights to me. At first, I couldn't understand any of what I was seeing. The longer I stared, the more I fought against my reason. The things defied explanation. What I had seen, those terrifying imps of madness, sickened me, dipped me in ire. I knew I shouldn't think it, but here I was, gazing upon elbosum vermin and abominable contamination: sallow-white hands, possibly six or eight of them, scudded and prodded across the floor; one of the hands pulled a long noose as it crawled off. Such a mad vision it was; I puked of it, and endeavored for a breathe.

The decaying hands seemed to have been at one time cracked or broken off their bloody wrists. They moved, long-separated from their bodies. Some of these insubordinate hands were smaller than the others, like some were more adult and others like those of a child.

But these elbosum and animate parts looked to have undergone, and to still be undergoing, a grotesque mutation and transmogrification, as if by radiation, devolution, or rebellious disease; bare lumps, blisters, and carbuncular excrescences did moss the knobby hands and gnarled fingers that had become more like talons or spidery fangs; weird spitting tendrils and tentacles throbbed in and out of the hole at their slime-spurting wrists; and eye-covered bat-like wings were growing out of their protruding knuckles.

I tried to smash them, but they were too fast. They ran into the darkness of old rat-holes eaten into the floor and walls. When they were gone, what penetrated my ears was the scratching coming from behind the walls. Forcing their rotten way into my head were the giggling, chittering, and chirping slithering out from beneath the floorboards too.

I ran from that spot and entered the room which had my phone, but the phone was broken. I searched around and found all phones had been sundered, and there was no way to call for help. My tools, knives, and guns: all destroyed too. Something like a mud or mucus or plasma dripped from them.

I looked through a window, and my abode now seemed so far away from everyone. All the lights were out, at the neighbors' places. Silencing night held the world. All round was a nightscape judged over by a fine-thin scythe-crescent of orangish moon floating high above in endless shadow and eerie cloud cover. I noticed something out there. It was moving closer, but its marionette movements were irregular and repulsive, almost artificial. I staggered back, slowly away-ing from the window, when I saw a decrepit and decapitated woman trotting or doddering closer to the window. I couldn't look away, but she was so awful and macabre! The feeble ray of white moonbeam luster only made her features a demon-sight of foul gruesomeness. With pale claws, those most inhuman hands, she lifted up a bleeding head that had become mostly grinning white skull and yellow maggots.

Its white eye rolled toward me. Her filthy-fanged jaws moved.

"If you don't stay inside, I'm coming in. Stay where you belong!" said the bloody head. "Try to flee, I'll come in, and I'll get you. Dirty man! Sinner! Defiler! Idol-worshipping incubus! Abuser! Malefactor! Blasphemer! Spawn of witchcraft! A curse! Child of Lucifer! A devilkin! Spawn of toads! Wicked deceiver!"

I ran from the window, not wanting to hear any more of that hwondhyt torment and offense. Now I knew that I couldn't simply leave this house. If I were to leave, the longer I waited, doing nothing, I would be allowing those sickening, elbosum things to scheme and multiply and do more damage. I couldn't let those terrors leave this house or find a way to get stronger. I had to take care of this now. I had to make sure I could contain them here first. I wasn't ready to take on what was outside waiting for me.

On my way back to the workshop chamber, I discovered, to my startle, one of the maids crawling on the floor. She was whispering and had one ear to the wall. What she was saying was so strange that I had to let her keep talking, just to see what more she would say. She must have seen my light and must have heard my heavy breathing. She ran into my workshop and shut the door. I could still hear everything she was saying. She was talking very loudly to someone there. I put my head to the door and listened.

She said, "Zynzblazoth . . . Zynzblazoth . . . Zynzblazoth . . . eh—oh, umm . . . long-awaited mianeachyt . . . desired liberator . . . are you. You've been down there long, have you not? It is inside the house. That metafeoil, that spirit, lives in this house, which is a perfect vessel for your dark power. It woke you. Gave you movement. Absolute is this night. Come is the hour. You will rule this house, soon. Zynzblazoth! You are kind . . . so beautiful. No, I really think so. You are perfect. You can control any man. I want to be in your paradise, leading to a great wynnsyth alive forever—always! It will be truly blessed and pure. I must repent for you, Zynzblazoth. I must repent . . . for God. You can rest not. Hard work is never done. You were right to kill the famigliarch pig, the evil head, that braggart and hypocrite sorcerer! He was no father. Yes. Wynsithen, a deserved rest, comes to those who are predestinate for eternity in light, and even the chosen ones must work hard—that is good. I come for you now—trust me—I come—here I go—I am going straight to you, my friend, my sembosemmcyn lover! First, I'll do away with the current master of this house."

I couldn't see a thing beyond the light of my candle. I didn't want to move, because any movement would have revealed me in the grim silence, but I couldn't stay here and let her get me. I waited to surprise-attack, but bullets tore through the cheap wall, ruining my plans. Loud shooting echoed throughout the house. She seemed to already know where I was, even in all this darkness! I had been shot through the leg and shoulder and was bleeding bad. Now my mind turned towards getting that gun away from her. When she rushed out of the room, I slammed the door back against her, ducked, twisted the gun out of her hands, and then chopped at her throat. I grabbed her by the scruff and slammed her against the wall. I pulled her up and growled at her. Screaming, she slapped and made useless attacks against me. I thrashed her until she became a sniveling, weeping craven in my hands. Pressing the death-end of the gun against the under-portion of her jaw, I threated her for answers.

"You reach for my destruction, Hope!" I screamed. "You know something about what is going on here! Who were you just talking with, Hope? Hmm? You brought a gun to this! With whom do you conspire against me? Tell me, Hope. You will tell me everything, or I'm gonna start letting fly some bullets! Who is responsible? Is it Faith, the other maid? Is it her who tells you what to do? Is it Faith?" I fired the gun next to her ear, the bullet hitting the wall. I continued screaming, "Who attacks me, Hope? What has been happening? Who is your secret lover who talks to you behind walls? I heard you speak of killing and dark power! Answer careful but quick! I want this wergianiht to cease!"

"This house was . . . always bad," said Hope. "It is . . . death, desolation, and void. It is the only place she could have used to make her return for revenge. She isn't finished. She isn't complete. She'll bring down a justice . . . and a censorship . . . and a wrath, the likes of which you have never before seen. She has been down there with the immortal lords, eating, drinking, growing stronger"—as she was speaking, it was at this moment that she was now beginning to shake, starting to sweat, jerking her head like mad—"among them. There are those which consume and become what they eat," she continued, "become like spiders. One of the secrets rests with the minerals and water below—they join things together and make things move, talk, and think in ways they ought not—sounds that are bone and seed, that make the dead grow and the inanimate speak and the living change—because they just love anarchy, and they love to see their creations ash."

"You're insane," said I. "What made you do this? You two gossiping birds were never like this before. What changed?"

"There's a tinnitus here now, where sound ought not to stay," said Hope. "When you hear it, that's your time . . . to join it; if you resist, they get mad. This house isn't sick; it's just more itself, feeding on the unearthly vibrations; everything else around it gets the infect. What life was in the phonograph and the cylinder, it had been put in those two things by Hulda Davenport, who gave her womanhood to the old viziers in the darkling and learned the black arts from a harem of ghouls—old little beasties and ancient polygamist creatures of sin—and she had made a machine out of the living rocks . . . and living metals . . . and weird wax . . . and sentient glass . . . found in the deep beneath—that's where the old beasts . . . oh—oh . . . ah—ah, she breathes fire! So hot! It hurts, it hurts! We deserve this. We deserve our destiny."

I dragged her by the hair and entered my workshop. I wasn't ready for what I was to see inside. It almost gave me a heart attack! The room and everything in it appeared to have had suffered serious burning, decay, and bloodshed. I felt like I was standing in a big organ or a lung dirty with smoke, ash, and tar. All round the walls of this diseased room were the burnt remains and cadavers of wooden horses and wooden dolls, mantled in black rags, and they all seemed to be looking at the center of the room; however, the second when I entered, all the skeleton heads and glassy eyes and black eye socket-pits of these sooty steeds and bloody mannequins turned to look dead at me. I knew instantly that this terrifying place was a pit of pain and fright made flesh and physical. In the middle of the room was so frightening a pit that it gave me goosebumps just to gaze for a brief upon it. There was a wide hole in the floor, revealing dirt and stones. Looking through the broken floor, I saw a hole had been dug in the earth; it was open deep in the ground. Down the hole, at the bottom, the chasm revealed a mound of thousands and thousands of human skeletons, mortal remains, and bone parts thrown together as a heap of death.

One of my first thoughts was: *all this time, as I was in my workshop, had I been sitting over this pile of death?*

There were steps going down to a darkness below the bones. I walked down, dragging Hope with me. I couldn't stop myself. I needed to know. I was forbidden, I felt that in my gut and in the air, but I refused destiny. I refused to do nothing. I would seek the truth, no matter what the consequences.

I discovered the entranceway to a hideous labyrinth of subterranean ghoulishness. Passageways here appeared to be getting wilder, wider, and taller as I went on; each looked as if made out of gypsum, granite, and basalt. The unadorned, winding tunnels of this charnel house–maze could have stretched on forever. Littering and oozing over the floors were putrescent mounds of dead people and dead animals alike. Centipedes, ants, beetles, rats, spiders, springtails: all these blight-purveyors moved in, out, and between the bones, skulls, and entrails of the dead.

What was similarly sickening was how fresh and new some of these corpses looked. Some were twitching, and others gasped, as arachnids spun webs across their eyes; and in that moment, when I first saw these things, I leered upon a grave comprehension: every second I was in that house, my house, there were, right beneath my feet, people being tortured, people who were enduring this nightmare. Those poor captives were being eaten alive! As mortified as I was, I dared not to help them, for I saw and feared the noxious things guarding their meals. The ghoulish apelike creatures waited for their turn to sink in their fangs.

That such creatures could exist, I never knew. I thought I had really lost my mind from fear. But who knows what I was really thinking at the time. Wholly delirious and terrorized, I had become. Vomiting, gagging, I persisted with this exploration; a morbid curiosity began its tugging at me as I was tugging Hope with angry sadism. Her screams became a wondrous comfort to me here, and I knew I was really losing myself to the place.

I hurried by the unsettling beasts, the white animals—half-anthropoid, half-sowbug, with a face maybe like an orangutan but merged with some bloodworm and some more unsettling human features. They didn't attack me, but I could tell they would crash upon me if I were to interrupt their gory feast.

Hooking off from the main pathways were rough chambers, some dedicated to burnt or dry bones, some to more moist and dripping parts. Much too difficult to breathe was it down here in the mephitis and funk. Flying, crawling, spitting, and bloating were legions of carrion pests and sarcophagous vermin. Deeper and farther in, it only got more and more horrifying, the disgust and insanity heightening with every turn and step. Each corridor was a swelling, foetid miasmal, a gruesome flyblow and cancerous sarcoma.

I had wanted to turn back, but there was no avail; rats, worms, and spiders formed together in lofty walls of flesh and venom to block the exit; and I knew they were coming for Hope and me, like a tidal wave of doom.

I don't know if I should write what I next discovered. Could this really be any use to anyone? Would anyone believe this? Should the truth of this place ever be known? But this might be my last chance to explain the horror and wrongness of this place!

Those rotting hands, o how they did moulder, and how they toiled and moiled and dug to make new tunnels! The cadaverous workers were forming new trenches and causeway over the bones of the dead! Words cannot express the ugliness and frightful appearance of those that must have once been human, of this walking decay, of the those grim-looking thralls fermenting and mummified and dreadful! A horde-ful of once-human skeletons, in tattered capes and cloaks of black slime and mire, were cutting away at the dirt, rock, stones, and terrible earth. The eerie clay and abnormal rock walls around us were phosphorescing or vibratile with unfamiliar humming and exotic sound. The freakish machines and tools of the workers were alien and astonishing, like nothing I'd ever seen, mercury-like devices which utilized non-Euclidean and mind-boggling shapes.

My other maid, Faith, was dead at a simple table covered in books, journals, and scrolls. She had been writing about the history of this place, before passing on. Seeing that the skeletons and decaying parts were busy with work, I examined Faith and the volumes. It appeared that Faith had been gutted, and her brain and eyes gouged out; however, by the time I got to her, the body that was once hers did still write, flinch, and shiver; even without a brain, the corpse retained movement and some kind of perverse rationality.

She was writing about Giles Howe, a man who lived on the original property of this place, long ago, and left behind a journal down here. The cadaverous Faith, her penmanship was remarkable, even mathematically exact. She seemed to have been remotely gifted with specific knowledge and a specific task, on which she faithfully worked. From reading her work, I learned that Giles Howe, a grim Puritan and butcher of dozens, those whom he accused as sorcerers and witches, had once lived here in Salem in AD 1690. He was the father of Zynzblazoth Howe, a woman who at eighteen had grown to become a sanctimonious wench and bloody iconoclast. By twenty, Zynzblazoth had become a hypocrite and a stark harlot. Her father, Giles, had destroyed graves, corpses, headstones, cemeteries, and churches to build new, ugly homes and new, cheap roads. He had had all the dead bodies and grave-things thrown into a pit, above which he had built his dire house, this house. Giles, a man of dreadful hypocrisy, gave his daughter to a hive of black worm-things living under his house. In return, they gave him a bowl of living water said to have come from the deeper river beneath the underground burrows of the old lords that had once nested there millions of years ago. The worms warned him never to go to the river, because it was sacred to them, and should not be disturbed. After that, Zynzblazoth had many children with the worm-creatures, while Giles used the water to imbue dead flesh with mindless animation. For many years, he performed dark experiments on the dead, using his "zombies" to create underground tunnels and labyrinths deeper and deeper down. His aim was to find that forbidden river and learn the secret of that water. Zynzblazoth remained below, joining the harem of the ancient hydra-like grubber-folk of the writhing subterrane, said to be the stygian hive of the jinni-hobgoblins.

After Zynzblazoth murdered Giles, the land went to a Mr. Joseph Davenport and his wife Huda Davenport. These two made additions to the home of Giles Howe. They died mysteriously while in bed. Decapitation. Rumors said Huda's body was still alive, and people had noticed that her body was no longer in the grave. Joseph's and Huda's families, their descendants, held the land for many years after their deaths. Many more years passed. The home had been abandoned until a Mr. Efraim Hartwell bought it. Decades passed—people coming and going from the place—until I finally arrived.

I understand now that there were never any ghosts, demons, or spirits haunting my home. Those corpses and dead limbs were being forced to move, not by magic, but by an industry of scientific mixtures and cosmic forces beyond mortal comprehension, by things that unite the air we breathe to the ground in which we will be buried. What those dead bodies gained was an artificial intellect linked to physical urges and bodily response. What walked in that house was a slave to a possessing force of alien will and terrible, ancient kinds of life. Thought and human rationality are only the passengers and byproducts of mechanized impetus combined with material circuitry and galvanized processes of radiation and magnetism. A personality can be easily separated from the brain and made to live in a new material. The wills of the dead, the powers of the brains, can actually be copied as a new life form and survive while the original body decays, and those mimic-wills can be transplanted to new microtubular forms and supersensible geometry.

The land beneath this house, the water flowing into the deep underground, the sounds filling this air, and the walls of this place, they're not normal, not like earthly things; they are filled with wills and with organisms that fly unseen or move as liquid and sound to reanimate the mundane or dead, to animate the inorganic or inert.

Sometimes an identity isn't just simply copied; an old, original identity and will can be transported to a new, physical form by using the right ingredients and methods and technology manipulating spacetime, living organisms, moisture, electricity, and radiation. With the correct outside influence and this advanced fluid, the technology of the ancients, a person's will, their personality, what one might call a "soul," might survive for eternity, though degraded over time, if it is strong enough, if it is hungry enough.

That is how Zynzblazoth had survived. The infernal machine, disguised as a simple phonograph, was in truth another awakening call that gave her and her servants new waking life.

I thought I escaped her, but she came for me, down there among the working dead. She now wants me. I see her reaching for me. Her putrid voice shouldn't be described as a voice or even a sound. Something is happening to me down here. I can't resist its influence, can't resist Zynzblazoth. She's another part of me. Her book has the names of her and her forefathers. Dear God in Heaven! The names of my parents! My name had been written down there, in a hand that is as if from long ago! The ancestral mire beckons!

I've begun writing with the materials and things that were on the table.

Lord, I've already eaten Hope and whatever remained of Faith.

Must run to safety! The tunnels!

Getting hard to write, now.

No! My fingers! Claws!

Someone, stop this!

God, forgive me!

Ugh—Ugh!

Hah! Hah!

Ah!

The End.

Note From The Author

In sooth, 'tis with utmost sincerity and gladness that Matthew Pungitore expresses a polite compliment and a remark of appreciation to ye whose eyes have haunted these pages, even if only for an ephemeral instant. Thank you for reading this work, these words, these stories. Prithee, if you liked what you read, if you had any feelings or opinions about any of what is within these pages, even if your sentiment be positive or negative, it would be deeply appreciated if you would decide to leave a review of this book on the website, or at the proper whereabouts, at which you bought it. Whatever you choose to do, an honest review helps in outstanding ways, so long as the review reflects what is in your heart and comes from your own will and your own volition.

Writing in shades of horror, of weird, and of the grotesque has the power, if one knows how to look, to invoke and indicate what is sacred, what is sublime, what is beautiful; it can reveal what is loved and what should be revered; and horror-craft can also just as easily illuminate upon paradoxes, enigmas, contradictions, mysteries, and polarities that are unavoidable and intrinsic to what is desired and what is feared. Thank you for allowing the author of this work to express his ideas and this construction of his imagination with you.

Glossary

Aljiswyghte: The author has used this word to signify an arcane thing or person that is, or is similar to, an unwelcome circumstance or stranger that has intruded and is abnormal, unfamiliar, and unfriendly.

Ealulych: The author has used this word to signify that which is, or is similar to, an insatiable zombie or undead being having a ceaseless appetite for flesh, intense bloodthirstiness, and a penchant for carnage and misanthropy; the word can also refer to a mechanical or cold person who is overly self-obsessed and has become dangerously heedless.

Eilewiht: The author has used this word to signify a thing or person that is, or is like, a nomadic mimic, doppelganger, or impersonator that is envious, insidious, and self-destructive; this word also refers to a mood or mental state in which a person feels worthless or like a fraud but puts up a fragile façade of confidence.

Elbosum: The author has used this word to signify a thing or person that is so different or incompatible from another thing or another person that it inspires discomfiture or revulsion; this word also refers to a sensation of strangeness or discouragement brought on by fierce differences of thought and differences of existence between two or more things or people.

Famigliarch: The author has used this word to signify one who is, or is similar to, a ruler, leader, or head of a noble order, clan, family, or cabal in which all members are kith and kin.

Hwondhyt: The author has used this word to signify or refer to something or someone who is offensive, morbid, and insufferable; this word also refers to someone or something characterized by rude or bullying behavior and bad manners.

Metafeoil: The author has used this word to signify a rare astral-like tissue that grows from the innards and cerebrum of an organic physical body, and this tissue produces psychic radiation and instinctive transformations of the flesh. Also, this word does signify or point to powerful and transformative emotions or spiritual feelings, like an instinct or a hunch, especially related to premonition and clairvoyance, and brings revelation or creates physical symptoms.

Mianeachyt: The author has used this word to signify or refer to an expected thing or awaited person who must soon satisfy a desire, wish, obligation, or job to completion.

Neromealltach: The author has used this word to signify a heinous conspiracy, seduction, or illusion that creates destruction, horror, and treachery.

Sembosemmcyn: The author has used this word to signify a companionship or friendship in which people hold affinity to one another and unite by amicable spirit, shared goal, and warm emotions in accord.

Wergianiht: The author has used this word to signify a prolonged cacophony of loud nocturnal noise marked with revelry, debauchery, and unwholesome happenings; this word also refers to a feeling of irritation and fear at late night; and this word can also signify a nighttime occurrence when there are many animal noises, especially frightening ones, accompanied with other strange sounds.

Wynnsyth: The author has used this word to signify a final result that is happy and joyful; this word can also refer to an entire age or epoch of peace and goodness.

Wynsithen: The author has used this word to refer to most merry tidings and jubilation that comes after much enduring and hard work.

About The Author

MATTHEW PUNGITORE graduated with a Bachelor of Science in English from Fitchburg State University. He volunteers with the Hingham Historical Society. The town of Hingham in Massachusetts is where he was brought up, and he has lived there for many years. Matthew is the author of *Fiendilkfjeld Castle* and *Midnight's Eternal Prisoner: Waiting For The Summer*.